Riding Solo

with the

Golden Horde

Riding Solo

with the

Golden Horde

A Novel by Richard Hill

The University of Georgia Press   Athens & London

Published by the University of Georgia Press
Athens, Georgia 30602
© 1994 by Richard Hill
All rights reserved

Designed by Kathi L. Dailey
Set in Bodoni by Tseng Information Systems, Inc.
Printed and bound by Thomson-Shore, Inc.
The paper in this book meets the guidelines for
permanence and durability of the Committee on
Production Guidelines for Book Longevity of the
Council on Library Resources.

Printed in the United States of America

98 97 96 95 94 C 5 4 3 2 1

Library of Congress Cataloging in Publication Data

Hill, Richard, 1941 Oct. 15–
    Riding solo with the Golden Horde : a novel / by
Richard Hill.
        p.   cm.
    ISBN 0-8203-1608-3 (alk. paper)
    1. Teenagers—Fiction.   I. Title.
PS3558.I443R5   1994
813'.54—dc20   93-5334

British Library Cataloging in Publication Data available

"Ol' Man River," written by Jerome Kern and Oscar
Hammerstein III, © 1927 PolyGram International
Publishing, Inc. Copyright renewed. All rights reserved.
Used by permission. "Work Song," by Nat Adderley
(music) and Oscar Brown Jr. (words), © 1960, renewed
1988 by Upam Music Co., a division of Gopam
Enterprises, Inc. Used by permission. The quotations
from *Down Beat* are reprinted with permission from
Down Beat.
19.95

*This work of fiction is dedicated to the memory
of two extraordinary musicians: Christine Baker,
whom I had the good luck to know, and
Gene Quill, whom I knew only through his work.
I dedicate it also to the memory of the writer
and teacher Michael Shaara, who helped a young
musician manqué find another form of expression.*

For Judy Amaron Hill.

*Special thanks to Elizabeth Little, Byron
Chapman, and Melton McLaurin.*

They're writing songs of love, but not for me.
A lucky star's above, but not for me.

—"But Not for Me," George and Ira Gershwin

Writing about music is like dancing about
architecture.

—Thelonious Monk

Music is your own experience—your thoughts,
your wisdom. If you don't live by it, it won't come
out of your horn.

—Charlie Parker, quoted in Gary Giddins's PBS
documentary "Celebrating Bird: The Triumph of
Charlie Parker"

I've never read one [novel about jazz] from the
musician's angle. They're all written from the
outside.

—Billy Taylor, interviewed by Don Gold
in *Down Beat*

If I cry a little bit when first I hear the truth,
don't blame it on my heart, blame it on my youth.

—"Blame It on My Youth," Edward Heyman
and Oscar Levant

Acknowledgments

A first draft of this novel was written at the Virginia Center for the Creative Arts. Another draft was written at Yaddo. The author wishes to thank these organizations for succor and sanctuary. He also wishes to thank Peggy Zangulo Quill, jazz scholars Charles Buhrman, Paul Burgess, Pat Chamburs, Dr. Alfred Finck, George E. B. Morren, Jr., and Dave Franklin, and also saxophone master Phil Woods.

Contents

Riding Solo

with the

Golden Horde

Summertime

Vic Messenger became aware, slowly, that he was awake, that he was ill, that it was already late in the day, that he felt some obscure new source of heat in his bedroom. The sun cooked a resinous perfume from the pine paneling and from the cedar chest under his south window. Normally he liked it, but this was not a normal morning. Whatever he'd done seemed to have poisoned him to his very roots—not a mere headache but a sickness of the soul. He heard a lawn mower somewhere and the Doberman, Senator McCarthy, barking at it. He knew he must open his eyes.

His mother, the new source of heat, stood at the foot of his bed. "Where's your horn?" she asked. She had a frown that looked like someone pretending to be angry, but he knew she was not pretending. "Probably in my car," he mumbled, his forehead and temples throbbing with the effort, a solid pain at the base of his skull as if someone had planted a knife there.

"Where's your car?" she asked.

Then he got up, panicked, the blood rushing to his head and tipping him over against the Magnavox—whose turntable was for some reason still in motion, its needle arm bouncing against the end of his *Chet Baker Sings* album. He put the arm in its cradle and turned off the hi-fi, then grabbed his jeans and thrust his feet into them, trapping his feet so that he fell into the open closet and hit his head against a music stand. He lay there for a moment, almost grateful for a specific pain to replace the oceanic hangover malaise. "This has got to stop," his mother said.

He brushed his teeth, gagging, and washed his face. He wet his hair with Vitalis and tried to comb it, but patches were matted from sleep, and it was curly anyway and wouldn't comb out straight and gleaming and hip even on his best day. He swallowed some aspirin. His sister, Val, waited for him in the hall, but she saw how bad it was and withheld her usual sarcasm. His mom offered him a glass of orange juice as he passed through the kitchen. He didn't want it but he thought he could at least do that to reassure her, and he gulped it down.

Outside, with his cousin Little Kingman watching him from his yard next door and his father looking on from the garage, and probably his mother and sister too, he vomited it up. Senator McCarthy escalated his noise, lunging against his chain. "Boy," Little Kingman said, "you in trouble now."

Vic tried to pull himself together. He spit, then pressed his hands against his head as if to put everything back where it belonged, then spit again, then threw up more juice, and then a thick, sickly bile. He went over to the spigot, turned on the garden hose, and washed his mouth with it, hoping also to disguise his vomiting. After a while, he felt a lightness come to his head and stomach. Little Kingman had brought him a garage rag that wasn't too nasty, and he blew his nose. "You gotta help me find my car," Vic told his cousin.

Little Kingman thought it was a good idea at first. He was two years younger than Vic and was now driving Vic's old Crusaire, a Sears and Roebuck motor scooter modeled on the Italian Vespa. Little Kingman would be a sophomore this year, Vic's senior year of high school, and he automatically got social points for being with his older cousin.

But then the directions added up in Little Kingman's head and he said, "Vic, we can't go to niggertown, even on Sunday morning."

"Trust me," Vic said, counting on the enormous authority even a year's high school seniority carried and Little Kingman's long hero worship and sometimes downright foolish devotion to him. "And don't call it Niggertown. It's Frenchtown, and it's where the car is." The truth was, this was only Vic's best guess as to where he'd find the Olds, and the sax, assuming the horn was in it. The last thing he remembered was closing time at the Cypress Room, on the beach, and if he closed the Cypress Room on Saturday night, then he either drove home or to Jake's to jam.

They hummed down the rippled old brick of 5th Avenue South to 22nd Street, called Two-Two Street by those who knew, took a right, and headed south, first through an industrial neighborhood and across the Seaboard tracks and then into Frenchtown's main block, mostly deserted, with Saturday night littering the street, along the path from the Manhattan Casino to the Icehouse Dance Hall and Geech's Pig Meat Bar-B-Q just beyond. Across Two-Two Street from the Manhattan—which was two-storyed and had a New Orleans–style balcony, despite its name, with wrought-iron railings like musical notation—the Red Star market waited behind grilled security windows for Monday's business. Fatback, hog maws, pig's feet.

Even now in the unforgiving bright sunlight of a Sunday morning and through a hangover, the block made Vic feel alive. Like an adventurer, an explorer in an exciting foreign land. They heard a church choir over the buzz of Little Kingman's Crusaire. "Man," Kingman said over his shoulder, "if my daddy found out I'd even *been* down here he'd bust my ass." Big Kingman was a goofball, Vic thought, a bigot, a construction redneck. Vic had once convinced Little Kingman to stand an overnight vigil in the mosquito-ridden palmettos of Goose Pond, watching for a communist cell meeting behind the Japanese plant nursery. Little Kingman had been so badly bitten that he had to go to the emergency room. Big Kingman beat him with an actual horsewhip and made him stay in his bedroom for a month, and Vic had never played a prank on Little Kingman again.

They turned right on Tangerine and buzzed through a more residential neighborhood—a strange mix of well-kept lawns and freshly painted houses with bare, weathered, littered rental shacks. In Vic's neighborhood the houses were all either white frame or concrete block painted white, with aquamarine or coral pink trim and decorated near the front door with plaster marlins, flamingos, or palm trees. The porch of one of the shanties had been hit several times by cars failing to make the turn onto Tangerine from 18th Street and was permanently and severely tilted, but it was nonetheless crowded this Sunday morning with drinking men in various stages of adjustment to the real, daylight, sober Sunday world, softening that passage with a bagged bottle they passed among them. A sweet wine, Vic guessed—Thunderbird or Sly Fox or Mogen David—and he felt reassured and superior because he knew he would never drink in the morning, no matter how bad it got.

In that same telling Sunday morning light, Jake's Lounge looked like a concrete bunker that had been attacked not by bombs but by bottles and cans, sandwich wrappers, crumpled packs of Pall Malls, Camels, Luckies, Kools. Just beyond Jake's and a short distance up the road that met Tangerine at that corner, Vic saw his bronze fastback Olds and four young black boys, around ten or so, playing in and around and on it. One was pretending to drive it. Another rode shotgun, bouncing on the rolled and pleated black-and-white Naugahyde, pretending they were going somewhere. A third sat on the louvered hood, laughing through the front window, and the fourth had opened Vic's sax case and was pretending to play the Selmer alto that had cost his Aunt Glad more than five hundred dollars.

When the boys saw them they looked frightened, too frightened to run. Vic smiled reassuringly. He got off the Crusaire and looked in, and saw his keys hanging in the ignition. The boy with the horn seemed most afraid. "We was just pretendin'," he said, holding the gold-lacquered instrument out to Vic. "I didn't use yo moufpiece."

"It's all right," Vic said. He returned it to its case, which the boy had set on the curb, and zipped it up. "Y'all were just watching it for me."

They nodded and scurried away, smiling, relieved. Vic looked at Little Kingman and saw an expression of wonder on his face that such a scene should ever occur. But when Vic started the Olds, letting its dual glasspacks rumble as it warmed up, Little Kingman lost his look of innocent amazement and made Vic promise to drive b*ehind* him all the way home. A dark thunderhead had come up suddenly, eclipsing the sun. The wind was gusting and Vic could smell rain in it. Last night's debris began to whirl in little tornados. They could see the storm coming as Vic followed Little Kingman back along Tangerine, back through the main block of Frenchtown, across the tracks again, and safely home.

Stormy Monday

Hurricane warnings flying on the first day of school. Bertha, the storm's name was. Boca Chica High was an open Florida school, built on a single level except for the library and gym, with patches of grass between the wings. The corridors flooded anytime it rained much, which was often, and students waded barefoot, boys with pant legs rolled up, from class to class.

Home Room

Same bunch for the last three years, some of them with him since grade school. Most of the *M*s and a few *N*s—nothing in common but the alphabet. Excited chatter, Vic sitting in a white T-shirt behind his bop shades, firming up his identity for this last year. It was the people you'd known the longest who tried to hold you back, keep you from changing. The *M*s and a few *N*s who'd watched one another mutate like science fiction monsters almost overnight—shooting up six, seven, eight inches over a summer, developing breasts, acne, facial hair, sometimes even personalities— were the ones who eyed him sideways now, like some new kid, wishing Messenger wouldn't sit there behind those shades and act like somebody they knew he wasn't.

Mickey Moran leered at him. Bowlegged, pigeon-toed, red-headed, and ropy-muscled, Mick was the head beach rat and the school's number one badass. Vic had hung out with the rats his sophomore year when he needed to shake the Poindexter image his music and other lessons had gained him. They were tough poor kids whose fathers mainly worked the grouper boats and whose mothers waitressed. He'd drunk beer with them, had breakfast late at night in the Pelican Diner, had even gotten into enough fights to satisfy them he was OK. And driving the custom Olds his dad had bought him from the famous hot-rodder Johnny Sugden hadn't hurt. That and sandspur football, the unofficial kind the punks played in vacant lots overgrown with sandspurs and littered with broken glass. The rules there were as different from regulation football as the playing field, meaner but with an odd kind of fairness built into a code more like that of criminals than athletes. Play often stopped for smoke and beer breaks, and sometimes to run from cops the neighbors called. Nobody who played sandspur football—and some of them, like Bobby Simpson and Mick Moran, were great athletes—ever went on to play in sanctioned high school or college games. Nobody who played sandspur football needed to prove anything more.

Like Vic, Moran had a forged ID, though he was probably close to twenty-one anyway. He and two of the other rats had shown up at the Cypress Room one Saturday night that summer, and now they knew his secret. "Gimme a smoke," Mick said, his way of saying hello, and Vic took the risk and palmed him a Viceroy. "Last year," Mick said. "Get outta this hole." Maybe Mick could do it this year, now that he was taking all shop and DCT, which was on-the-job trade training. Get out and onto a grouper boat. Failing that, build houses. People kept moving here.

Static. Announcements: School canceled tomorrow if the storm hits. Cheers, applause. You couldn't pay these kids to miss school this time of year, this year, the biggest so far in anybody's life. Football practice, cheerleading tryouts, debate team, and a smorgasbord of other creep club meetings like chess and chemistry. An upbeat greeting from the principal about how the future began now. They were always saying that lately. In science classes, the GE and GM films promised a future of ever-better refrigerators, cars that drove themselves, maybe even, who knew, a heli-pad on every roof? Vic associated the word *future* with the ubiquitous voice of the Erpi Classroom Film narrator. Welcome to the fuuuuture, Now! Vic could tolerate it because he knew he wasn't in it anymore.

The homeroom teacher passed out their class schedules. Vic had Art, Phys Ed, Study Hall, English, Music Theory, and Band, a schedule designed for students bound, his adviser had told him, neither for college nor anyplace else she could think of. Vic told her that he had an audition at Juilliard in the spring, which was the truth, and she said he'd better hope it went well. Now he sat in homeroom, silently playing the opening riff and what he remembered of Charlie Parker's solo on "Now's the Time." The heels of his hands rested on his jeans and his fingers just barely moved in what he could figure of the fingering, though he was mostly faking it.

Hall Passage

Kids carrying their books, shoes, socks, dropping one, the other, laughing, shrieking when the waves they made in their passage lapped higher on their legs. Vic had an army surplus knapsack containing a notebook, his English text, a pencil, a pen, his cigarettes, always several copies of *Down Beat*, and always a conqueror book—a novel or history of Attila, Genghis Khan, Tamerlane, Suleiman, even Alexander. Lightly armed, fast-moving, hungry barbarians overrunning civilizations that had grown soft, ripe for picking. His sister Val, a junior, came up behind and frogged him on the arm. "You really think you're cool," she said. "But what you don't realize is that people think you're a freak and nobody will go out with you."

"I know how to find my own way out," he said. "Don't bug me." She made a face at him, like throwing up.

Art

Weird class—combination of skaters like him and serious students like Emily Dickinson, who was Vic's girl last year, he supposed, and who, if her luck held, might pass from high school, where most people had never heard of her namesake, to college, where most were too mature to kid her about it. And remain a lusty virgin. Vic hadn't called her all summer. He'd devoted a year to her seduction and failed, and he would no longer be satisfied with dry humping and hand jobs, especially if strings were attached.

Mr. Olivetti, the art teacher, was a secret drinker. Normally a tolerant and bemused presence in the classroom, he'd had two episodes in which he threw pastel chalk, styluses, and brushes, even jars of paint, at unruly students and had nearly been fired for it. Nearly but not, and the message was not lost on students, who pretty much did what they wanted but did it quietly, kept an eye on him, and didn't push it.

Vic reread a January *Down Beat* while Olivetti lectured on chiaroscuro.

Down Beat

WOMEN IN JAZZ: DO THEY BELONG?   ELVIS PRESLEY: ALL WASHED UP? "Jailhouse Rock" could be the straw to break the camel's back.   ART PEPPER: PROGRESS REPORT. The alto saxophonist is grimly determined to make a new life for himself. . . . a phrase in which the key word stands out in brilliant contrast to the living death of heroin addiction which entombed the altoist for some of the most vital years of his young manhood and musical creativity.   strictly ad lib: Johnny Richards and his orchestra start the new year with a two-week stand at Birdland   Coral has a Neal Hefti big band album in the works, sidemen including Jim Dahl, Bernie Glow, Gene Quill. . . . Cross Section Interview with Billy Taylor by Don Gold: NOVELS: I've never read one from the musician's angle. They're all written from the outside.

Vic had a secret behind his secret weekend sessions with Buster Cooper and the other cats, and it was that he thought an obscure white alto player named Gene Quill would become the best alto man in the history of the world. Quill had played with the Johnny Richards and Neal Hefti big bands and on so many recent recording and club dates that he was just about number one call on the East Coast—and not a flutist! Vic wasn't sure how he'd say it when the time came, if it ever did, but he heard something there that he thought was going to rise up and soar and leave Art Pepper, Bud Shank, Cannonball Adderley, the flawless, fluid grace of Paul Desmond, and even the great Charlie "Yardbird" Parker in the shade. And a still deeper secret was that he'd attached himself somehow to Quill's fate, not really understanding the process himself, so that if Quill could do it, so could he, or if he couldn't, at least he'd know what it took that he didn't have.

The bell rang. Emily Dickinson slipped him a note without looking at him. "Why don't you call me?" she'd written. "People are saying strange things about you. I know how to do something new that you'd like. And besides, who's going to help you with your senior English paper?"

Phys Ed

Calisthenics. Vic did them only when Coach Rudolph was watching him directly and therefore didn't need a shower. He wondered briefly during side-straddle hops what it was Emily had learned and who had taught her.

Study Hall

Hall pass. Library.

cereal helps you avoid "mid-morning letdown"   ELECTRIC REFRIGERATOR NEVER RUNS OUT OF ICE CUBES!

Sub-launched missiles and new detection methods bring big changes in U.S. tactics   the *full* flavor of fine tobacco—the kind the American Tobacco Company is famous for   The whole country hoops it up in a new craze   When the British army liberated Bergen-Belsen . . . I stood watching the naked bodies rolling into one of the huge pits   Scientists, bah! If they think they can convince God-fearing, God-loving Christian people that Adam and Eve were a couple of apes, they're crazy!   If Brigitte Bardot has really found true love   BIG FUSS OVER TV QUIZ SHOWS   Americans have a tendency to operate on a frontier theory when the frontier has long since ceased to exist   The most common complaints are of noise   BING'S BOYS ON THEIR OWN   THE BURNSES OBSERVE GRACIE'S RETIREMENT   Thursday is the day set aside for Negroes

Vic checked out a book called *Attila: The Scourge of God*. He read: "From what land did they come? Popular belief held that they issued from the very ends of the world. The Goths, who knew them well—having been driven by them from their own lands—told of how one of their own kings, Filimon, had expelled certain sorcerers who, fleeing to the deserts, had coupled with the demons of sand and wind. And from these unions was whelped a race of monsters, dreaded equally by the Emperors of China and by their neighbors to the west. Deserting their Asiatic home twenty or thirty years before, these mongrels had flung themselves at Europe. When asked their name, they replied with a resonant syllable like the neighing of a horse. Of their language nothing had been caught except this brief sound, *ioung*, which, tempered to Latin throats, passed for the name—Huns."

Lunch

Spaghetti, with bread and coleslaw and little squares of red Jell-O that a woman wearing a plastic glove was picking up from a cut mold and putting on each plate. The woman's hair was also wrapped in plastic, with a few brown strands showing. She was thin and not pretty. Vic was fascinated. "What's it like to do that?" he asked her. "I'll bet it's strange after a couple dozen or so." The woman began to cry and left the service line, and the other lunchroom women glared at Vic, the smart-ass, behind his shades.

His appetite spoiled by that misunderstanding, Vic ate a few bites and handed in the tray, then walked across the parking lot in a light drizzle to the Edge, literally the far edge of the lot, where Dean Batten allowed punks to smoke after lunch. As he neared the group, he sensed violence, one of those frozen scenes you can come upon among men and other animals in which something has been communicated and answered or not answered and everything is frozen in a tableau. When somebody moves, it will probably be bad.

Vic realized there was a new guy. He was short and dark and narrow-shouldered, had frizzy black curly hair, was wearing some weird Cuban-looking shirt and sunglasses, and carried a thermos bottle like some dork. He seemed to have held out a cigarette and asked for a light, innocent of local ritual, and now Mickey Moran was between him and the school, crowding him back toward the weeds and the railroad tracks and the Negro cemetery beyond, and the new cat didn't know whether, as Mick would put it, to shit or go blind.

"Here's a guy you oughta meet, Messenger," Mick said. "Another Dopey Gillis." The rats laughed. Vic laughed with them and felt the tension lessen. The new hipster was pale. His scared eyes weren't visible behind the shades, but his still unlit cigarette was shaking a little in his fingers.

"I know this guy," Vic said. "He's all right."

"What does 'all right' mean to you freaks?" asked little Junior Hazlewood.

"It means we're playing the Trafficante wedding Sunday," Vic said.

Junior wasn't buying. "What the fuck do *we* care?"

Vic thought of something that might make it so he didn't have to keep taking care of this new cat. "Well, he's Corsican," he said. "And you know what Corsicans do."

Junior shook his head and motioned with his hand like Go ahead and tell us but it's bullshit. Moran laughed, liking this new business.

"Corsicans tell Sicilians what to do," Vic said. "And we all know what Sicilians do."

Junior waited. Most of the rats were smiling now.

"Sicilians tell Italians what to do. And the Trafficantes are Sicilian and they kill people . . . a lot. So if this guy gets hurt and can't play that wedding, I don't think I can help you, though you know I'd try."

The bell rang and they walked back, Junior still grumbling and Moran laughing, really digging it. Vic dropped back with the new cat. "I'm Vic Messenger," he said, and held his hand out flat.

The new cat moved his own across it, sliding him skin so subtly that it almost felt like the wind. "I'm Basil Belheumer," he said. "Call me Baz. And I'm not Corsican, but I really do blow trumpet."

"I'll catch you in band, then?" Vic asked.

"Solid. And music theory?"

"Yeah. Later, then."

But Baz stopped in the lot. "That was too much what you did out there, man," he said. "I mean, that scene was the worst. I've heard smoking is bad for your health, but I didn't have eyes for dyin' *today*. Like, I've been meaning to learn to fight, man, but I don't want to hurt my chops."

"I try not to do it," Vic said. "But if I have to, I learned years ago to do two things. One: Grab his neck in a headlock and hang on. Two: Think of something weird to do."

"Like what?"

"Like the last time, I sang 'The Cattleman's Song.' Or maybe it's 'The Cattle Song.' You know, with Eddie Arnold yodeling. Then switched to 'Yipee ti ki yo, get along, little dogie.' Spooked the cat. He didn't want to fight me any more."

"A gas, man," Baz said. "But what key?"

They laughed.

"Let me offer you a taste," Baz said.

Vic stood in amazement as Baz took the top off the thermos and poured it full of what looked like orange juice. Vic drank his capful of screwdriver and returned the cap to Baz, who poured and drank one for himself. Then, his cool recovered, Baz said: "Later."

English

Mrs. Benoit had been his junior English teacher, too, and they had a secret understanding: He would read four serious books during the year and report on them. He would also do a senior paper. Otherwise, he would be quiet and read as he liked in class.

Swinging Scholarships. Two more scholarships to promising young musicians were announced . . . to the Berklee School, Boston.   Swinging Seminar. Twelve students will be accepted for what shapes up to be a swinging seminar on the Role of Jazz in American Culture.   On What Road? Excitement ran high in Greenwich Village. . . . the arrival at the Village Vanguard of Jack Kerouac, author of *On the Road.* Just what Kerouac would do on the floor of the star-showcase-turned– jazz spot was not clear.   Out of My Head, by George Crater: Mort Sahl says on a recent tour with Dave Brubeck they played Portland, Maine, on a Saturday night. After the concert, around midnight, Sahl and Paul Desmond got into a cab and said to the driver, "Take us to where the action is." Reports Sahl: "They took us to a place where they were fishing illegally."

Music Theory

In the choir room, for the first time, with Miss Cook, the tiny, feisty, legendary, and fiercely serious choir director. Baz was there, too. Miss Cook read through the roll, having a few words with each student. It was Vic's first contact with her.

"Mr. Messenger," she said in his turn. "I've heard about you, looked up your records. You've placed first in the last three state contests on your instrument. Do you know you also have one of the highest IQs in this school, and one of the lowest grade point averages?"

"No," Vic said, "but maybe if you hum a few bars I could pick up on it."

Dean's Office

Batten gave him detention, two hours after school, to be spent at Miss Cook's discretion.

Band

Mr. Branthooven was a very tall Ichabod Crane sort of man, very serious. He had gotten Vic his Juilliard audition and offers of several university music scholarships. Vic had played first chair since his sophomore year and had kept a fragile truce with the director, who lived in more or less constant fear of the kind of anarchy musicians, even the older ones, could cause—seemed, in fact, compelled to cause. Looking at this new Belheumer boy warming up, and with Jimmy Johanssen and his crazy hands and weird noises back on percussion and Dale Cleaver first-chair trombone and Vic himself, Mr. Branthooven expected the worst. And it began when he asked them to tune. "Please give me a concert B-flat," he said.

And in the already ancient tradition of band goofs, Baz, Johanssen, Cleaver, and Vic sang out: "Concert B-flat."

Detention

"You can't get out of this class," Miss Cook said. "There aren't any crib courses left for you to take, and you need theory for college, or anything you do as a musician. And I'm not going to let you leave. But if you screw around I'll have you in detention every afternoon for the rest of the year. No, don't say anything. There's really not much worse than a high school hipster. It's something fairly new, but I hate it already. You think you're the only one in town who ever listened to jazz or thought about a different way to live than we've got here? Listen to me. I lived in the Village. I went to parties with people who cut the records you're listening to. I had dinner with Charlie Mingus, at his place, and he came to my place for dinner. I knew Miles, I knew Bird, I knew all them cats. I got Bird's axe, man. I knew Basie before he could count, ain't that wild?"

Vic couldn't believe it. This from Miss Cook? "That's from Lenny Bruce—"

"It's on his album, but I think it's a Bob and Ray bit. 'Interview with Shorty Pederstein.' See, I'm hip, but you don't see me slouching around here in a beret. Save us both a lot of hassle. Grow up and stop sassing me. If you don't, I'll just farm you out to Dean Batten and he'll have you banging erasers with the other Neanderthals. If you do, I can teach you some good things. No, I'm not finished yet. I want you to read the novel *Doctor Zhivago*, by Boris Pasternak, and the novel *A Portrait of the Artist as a Young Man*, by James Joyce, and give me oral reports on them, in well-articulated speech and correct Standard English grammar. The first, eight weeks from now; the second, four weeks after that. The rest of this hour and the one you owe tomorrow you'll collate music sheets for me. And I want you to think about dumping art or study hall and joining the choir. You have a good baritone voice, almost a bass but not quite yet. Have you heard me and do you agree?"

"Yes, ma'am," he said, and enjoyed saying it.

"Tell me something. Why the barbarians? Those trashy books you're always reading in other classes?"

Vic didn't mind the question, but he didn't know how to answer. He found himself saying: "Simple. Simpler. Clean."

She nodded vigorously, assembling some pages and knocking them together on her lectern. "Just as I thought. Wouldn't it be simple just to have a horde or a hurricane sweep through, clear away all the complicated stuff? Tired of the button-down life? Become a world conqueror. You don't think Alexander and Attila's asses got sore? You use the word *clean* about people who covered their faces with animal grease and never bathed in their lives?" She paused. "You know the two things teenagers want?"

"Sex and liquor?" Vic was pushing it, but she didn't bristle.

"Anarchy and total control over their environment. Contradiction? Sure, but that's it. You go out and get drunk and try to figure things out in the backseat at the drive-in, then return to the perfect safety of your parents' home. Who could ask for a better life? Except . . ."

Vic waited.

"It doesn't last forever. This is the last year of that for most of you. Time to fly away, leave the nest, look for Birdland. Scary, right?"

He nodded.

"And you should be scared. I've seen it over and over. This last year, especially the last semester, accelerates. Too many choices or no choices, kids are about to be thrown out of here, too, expected to fly. They get scared, angry, desperate, and they're *always* horny. Kids make decisions over a weekend or overnight that dictate the terms of the rest of their lives. They look around when the dust has cleared and they're married, in the army, off to college, in jail, dead. One dumb, wild move and you're too far in to pull out, rolling too fast for the brakes to hold. It's like a hurricane, everybody looking for shelter. Some refuse to look, choose to ride the wind. I admire them, and I fear for them. That's life. Be careful these coming months. And don't buy that romantic bohemian crap about booze and drugs being part of enlightenment, nonconformity, necessary suffering, either. Life has plenty of suffering to go around. You don't have to go out looking for it. You can do anything sober. I've proven it."

Vic wanted to ask about that but thought he'd better let it go.

Home

Supper. Watch the news with Mom and Dad to digest, then an hour's practice, Senator McCarthy howling as usual. To bed to read. "The subjugation of the West was but a stage, and the fall of the Roman Empire would provide the wherewithal so necessary to his larger schemes. Once master of Asia, he would subdue Geiseric in Africa and, after having brought under the Empire of the Huns the whole Mediterranean basin, he would reign over all lands from the China Sea to the Pillars of Hercules. *He would become Ruler of the World.*"

La Bamba

Friday night he just went out cruising, sipping from a six-pack in his cooler, taking them one at a time from the trunk, returning the empties there, ready to toss any can within reach at the sight of a police car and gulp Listerine, but still enjoying the Olds, taking a turn in Sugden's legendary car around Triplett's, where the St. Pete High kids went, and Crossroads, a kind of neutral drive-in, and to the A, the A&W root beer drive-in where Boca Chica kids hung out. Vic could never have had such a car if his old man hadn't been in the business. He'd caught Sugden when he needed the money and a used pickup for his roofing business more than a car that he'd outgrown and his wife hated.

The only thing Vic had done to Sugden's Olds was to have the hood louvered and repainted and to replace the three two-barrel manifold and carburetors with a four-barrel one, for better gas mileage. Sugden had done most of his modifications using stock parts, putting a 1949 Olds cam and '52 rocker arms in the 1950 block, for higher lift. The hydramatic was beefed to the point that when it shifted it felt like God kicking the rear bumper, but though it was obvious to everyone who knew cars, it would show only if somebody protested at the drags and put up the money to tear it down and put it back together, and so far nobody had. Vic had won several trophies running in the stock class but had quit because so many angry greasers wanted to kick his ass. Besides, it really wasn't fair. The car was painted metallic bronze and had stiff shocks in the rear, and with the fastback shape it looked like a wedge cutting through the air in both directions. It had moon discs over the hubs—smooth, tooled, blank aluminum disks bought from the J. C. Whitney catalog—and lake plugs—chrome muffler bypasses that you could open at the drags.

He fiddled with the dial and got WLAC in Tennessee, sponsored by Randy's Record Mart of Gallatin and the makers of White Rose petroleum jelly. Ray Charles, B. B. King, John Lee Hooker, Jimmy Reed, Bobby "Blue" Bland. The later it got, the better the reception. Some nights he got Latin stuff from Cuba. Weekdays it was WTMP in Tampa, with Ernest "Country Boy, Rockin'" Rogers from Cheraw, South Carolina, and "Tiger Tom" Hankinson spinning the records, and on Sundays the Reverend "Goldie" Thompson presented groups like The Mississippi Blind Boys and The Gospel Owls. Off and on they'd let a guy named Pat Chamburs play jazz on WDAE, a mainstream AM station. He was hip and had crickets named Clyde and Fern on the show, or cricket sounds, and later he was on a little station on Tierra Verde, WILZ, and played a lot more jazz there, and somebody said he went off to New York with the girl who became Lauren Hutton.

He parked after his last beer and dumped all his empties discreetly into the garbage can behind the A. He ordered a cheeseburger with mustard and pickle only and a root beer float. He ate and drank and talked to a few people who stopped by. The only interesting rumors were that Emily was going out with Billy Glover, who seemed to be smiling a lot, and that Crump the cop had asked about him. Sometimes hip paid off.

Crump hated teenagers, especially hated the idea that they could drive, especially that they could drive cars like Vic's, especially that they drank beer as they drove them. He'd arrested Vic once for possession of alcohol as a minor but couldn't make drunk driving stick. It had made a bad scene at home. His dad, who worried less about drinking than his mom, nearly kicked him out, but his mother, who feared it more than anything, had talked his father out of the expulsion. "God knows what he'll do if we're not watching." The kids called Crump Creep, or Crapp, or Clunk, or Dump, or Officer Krupke.

Vic was headed home, vaguely thinking about buying a couple of singles, when he saw the flashing light. He chugged Listerine from the under-the-seat bottle and pulled over. Crump always took his time, inspecting the car for violations first—a bad bulb, a bald tire. He always wrote Vic a muffler ticket, and Vic paid it and had stock mufflers put on at Pete's Pure Oil and had it inspected, then had the glasspacks restored.

"Get out of the car," Crump said. Then Vic followed the usual drill, walking the line, closing his eyes and touching his index fingers together, Crump smelling his breath. "I've stopped you so many times I hate the smell of Listerine," Crump said. Vic didn't answer. "Open the trunk."

Vic did, and the cooler was empty but still cool. "Always on the edge," Crump said. "Muffler violation."

Vic said, "Yes, sir."

"But I'm gonna get you for a lot worse. That's what makes my job interesting."

Vic didn't answer back.

"And you know why I'm gonna get you?"

Vic was silent.

"Because," Crump said, "I know a lot more about you now. Where you go, what you do, all the things you don't want people to know. Like your car's been seen in Niggertown."

Vic felt a vacuum inside, suddenly frightened and hollow, only faintly angry, way back behind the fear.

"What are you doin' in Niggertown?" Crump asked, his face close, his own breath smelling of coffee and decay.

"I'm afraid I don't know that term, officer," Vic said, his mouth suddenly very dry, his breathing shallow, a melting sensation on the backs of his arms and legs and along his ribs.

"It's where niggers live," Crump said.

Vic wanted to say . . . didn't say anything. He tried to turn away. "Stay right where you are," Crump said. "I could do a lot to you right now that you couldn't prove, things that don't show, or accidents you might have had down in Niggertown."

Vic was trembling now. If Crump didn't stop soon he would have to do something.

Crump began writing the muffler ticket. He handed it to him. "Watch your ass, boy," he said and returned to his car.

He waited behind, forcing Vic to calm himself and drive away first, his leg jumping from adrenaline on the accelerator, making it hard to do smoothly. He made the turn toward his house and Crump followed. He turned in at his alley and Crump turned, too. Then Crump stopped and waited for Vic to park in the carport. Vic opened the door so the interior light would go on and closed it again, then waited to see how long Crump would stay. After a minute or so Crump backed out and headed north.

Vic walked two blocks down the dirt and shell alley—soaked with oil to keep down the dust—to the Bethwood Tavern, a neighborhood bar on 5th. It was his ace in the hole and he didn't like to test his ID there often, so close to home, but the bartender studied his ID and his face, shrugged, and sold him two cans of Miller's to go. He drank them in the alley walking back.

Then he washed quietly so as not to wake his parents and went to bed, using the earphones his cousin Georgie the electrical genius had rigged so he could listen without bugging anybody. The last two beers were a warm comfort in his body, a pleasant tingle in his head, a permission to leave behind the world of Crump.

He played Johnny Richards's *Wide Range* album with Gene Quill's great solo on "The Ballad of Tappan Zee." Vic was staking it all on this: If a human being could play like that, everything else must melt before him. Nobody could hassle him, arrest him, do anything but love him for this gift of flight. Or if they didn't love him, why should he mind? He was untouchable, above technique, singing in a voice that wasn't a saxophone any more but was instead his true soul's song, the sax only what the word *instrument* implied—a tool, a lever on a point of real gravity to launch the flight. If a man could play like that, then there was a God, or at least there was love. Someone had played the solo for Charlie Parker, and Parker was quoted as saying it wasn't possible for a human being to play that way. Maybe he was just sleepy and a little juiced, but then maybe that was how you had to be to think about art and God, forget Miss Cook.

But Parker, one of the first to fly, had crashed, not in flames but out of fuel. They said the medical examiner estimated him to be around fifty-six years old when he died at thirty-four. Vic feared that there was some dark deal you had to make, a pact with the devil. He feared that he was prepared to make it. He'd read mythology in junior high—about Prometheus, who stole fire from the gods for humans to use and spent eternity chained to a rock with his liver being eaten by buzzards or something; and Daedalus and his son, Icarus, who flew too close to the sun and fell when his wax wings melted. Maybe it was something like this: To bring joy you had to suffer, pay a price. The more joy, the greater the suffering required. That was where the blues came from, folks singing in their chains. You made good out of bad, which meant you had to have the bad, go out and find it if you didn't have enough. But you always risked coming too close, pushing too hard, and losing it all. Maybe Parker didn't run out of fuel so much as poison himself with it, but at least he got to fly. Vic feared he'd make the deal and never get off the ground. Maybe Miss Cook was right: Only drunks bought into this romantic crap, and novelists. They either exaggerated the suffering or played it down so you never thought of Attila as having a bad case of chapped ass.

But maybe in order to find the truth of it he would first have to put it into words, or have someone help him make a verbal map of the territory to conquer and the path into it over the mountains, like the Karakoram Pass across the Roof of the World that the Moghuls had come through. Maybe that was why musicians used words so carefully. And so, maybe Miss Cook was right. Maybe the trick was to handle life like a jazz number, whether it was based on a standard or a riff—take off on your own and fly if you can, move back and let the others try their wings, trade four bars, eights, but everybody comes together again safe on the out chorus. Takeoff. Landing. No casualties. But what *did* you use for fuel? How could Miss Cook stand there and assure him that he could make black magic with the little old baby's-ass-pink soul that he was?

Vic expected it to be harder, almost impossible—thus the magic, the deal with the devil. He also wanted it simpler. He read: "Wandering poets sang of his adventures, and the narratives of his glory followed the slow rumbling march of the Hun chariots. The destroyed cities rebuilt their walls; the field wherein 'grass should never grow again' yielded new harvests. While the body of Attila slowly decomposed under its burden of treasures, the luminous halo born of legends formed about his name.

"And perhaps a young chieftain of the horde was already dreaming of stretching forth an invincible bow to the four corners of the world, and speeding his horsemen on the road to another Great Conquest."

The Preacher

When he got up on Saturday his mom had taken his sister to her clarinet lesson and his dad was talking to himself in the bathroom mirror. He probably hadn't closed the door because he never expected Vic up so early. Once he'd seen it, Vic was afraid to move for fear of shaming him and thus became a captive audience.

"So here's how it is, Baby Ross," his dad was saying. "You bird-dog any more of my deals for that cousin of yours and I'm gonna drag your sheeny ass into the alley for a nose job, the hard way." His father shook off that version and started again, then sensed Vic's presence and turned, and shook his head, embarrassed. "Never mind this," he said. "I'm not going to last at Ross Ford. Ross's kid's stealing my deals for one of their relatives, a new kid. Never mind that sheeny business either. My best boss was a Jew, back in Philadelphia. I was just practicing what I'm gonna say. A little satisfaction."

He gave Vic the bathroom. By the time Vic finished washing, he was gone. Vic practiced most of the morning, Senator McCarthy yowling. At times during the exercises he felt like crying and had to stop. He'd never seen his father that way, could never have imagined him so weak. He remembered his father playing the piano, "It Had to Be You," something he hadn't done since Vic got big enough to reach the keyboard. When his dad got home, Vic went out and found him in the garage, winding new line onto a casting reel.

"You could sell my Olds," Vic said.

"Why do that?"

"Didn't you quit?"

"Sure I quit, but I got hired back at Riggins Brothers. We're going bass fishing tomorrow. A car man like me can always work in this town. I've been at Ross three times, and I'll probably be there again. Nothing's permanent in the car business. So why sell the Olds?"

"I thought we might need the money. And it's conspicuous. Crump spends his life following me."

His dad paused and bit the line in two. "Here, make yourself useful and hold this rod." He fed the line through the eyelets on the rod. "Can you blame him? He caught you drinking. It's against the law. It's driving your mother crazy. It ain't part of childhood to drink. It worries me, too."

"I know. I usually don't juice unless I'm playing somewhere."

"Somewhere you're too young to be anyway. The musician's life kills people a lot older and smarter than you."

"It's not so bad."

"Who you think you're talking to, kid? I'm not Ozzie Nelson here. Who do you think bought those Art Tatum seventy-eights you listen to, the Freddy Slack boogie-woogie stuff, the Basie and Ellington and Goodman and Dorsey records you grew up on? Harry James, Krupa, Kenton. You think the Record Fairy left those?"

"I forgot."

"See, your memory's going and you're only eighteen. I played a little piano. I made a dime once upon a time."

"You don't play any more. I haven't heard you since I was little."

"You're still little, junior, and I could quit playing because *I* only played a *little* piano in the first place. If I'd gotten good enough to want it, Christ knows where I'd be now. I count it a blessing that I always knew I was never good enough to do it right."

"But how'd you know? And why not play now?"

His father paused, using a knot as an excuse. "I knew. And because it hurts," he said finally. "I'd like to keep you from hurting. That's what parents are for."

"Why the lessons, then? Tap, acrobatics, ballet, piano, clarinet, sax, flute? I had to learn to fight because they called me Liberace."

"Your mom's idea. Mrs. Messenger's Trained Performing Human Children. Next stop Broadway and Ed Sullivan. She wanted you in the spotlight, and now she knows what people do when they're in the light and the stage fright gets them, and she's scared to death you'll end up in a wet ward or dead with a needle in your arm. I mean she's *really* scared. Maybe if you'd chosen a different instrument. Now, drummers, for example, are all flipped, but they live for*ever*. You teach a man to play the alto or tenor saxophone, you might as well turn over the hourglass 'cause that's about how long he'll last. I don't know what it is about that horn."

"I'm sorry."

His dad had an old plug with the hooks removed that he used to practice casting. They walked outside and he whipped it down the oiled alley, into Mrs. Latta's garbage can lid. Senator McCarthy started barking again.

"That dog was a mistake," his dad said. "But I'm afraid if he senses I want to get rid of him he'll tear out my throat."

Vic laughed.

"Here's an idea," his father said. "Big Pinhead Kingman's going to buy Little Pinhead Kingman an old forty-nine Ford pickup. I offered him a couple nice cars, but he's buying it off some cracker he works with. We'll buy back the scooter for thirty bucks, and when you want to go someplace inconspicuous and legitimate, you ride that. You could strap your horn on like before."

"I'll look like a dilbert."

"And Crump won't bust you because he'll know you can't carry anything much to drink on it, and you also can't ride it drunk or you'll bust your head."

"So when I take the car I can't drink because Crump will get me, and when I want him to ignore me I can't drink because I'm on the scooter."

"There you go. Deal?"

"What choice do I have?"

Another pause. "I'll be honest with you. I love you, and your mother does, and even your sister does. But if you keep it up you have to go, no matter what your mom says. If you choose that life, we can't stop you, not for long, but I will stop paying for it."

"OK. I'm sorry. I love you too."

His dad turned away. "Do me a favor," he said, after clearing his throat. "Take that crazy motherfletching dog on a leash and get that old Schwinn of yours I fixed and run his ass until his jaw hangs down and he can't bark any more. And see can you get a truck to run over him."

He found Baz at the Cypress Room bar, sitting next to Mad Moped Max, the now-sober former rocket scientist— he claimed—who rode a moped and went to bars to hear music. Max had good taste in music and some interesting crazy ideas, and did not, in fact, drink anything but Coke or ginger ale. The smoke was already heavy, the tables already occupied, and the bar smells of malt, cut fruit, perfume, cologne, and disinfectant gave Vic the already familiar tingle of anticipation. Over by the bandstand there'd be the exotic odors of valve and key oil, cork grease, hair tonics, whiskey, and spit, and more stale and fresh smoke—the smell of jazz.

He'd decided to drive the Olds and not drink much, and maybe Mad Moped Max was a good omen. Maybe riding the moped was how Max stayed sober. He wore a close crewcut and stayed pretty pale, though he lived on the beach, and had a sarcastic way of talking to people, like a high school science teacher who thought the kids were stupid. Vic ordered a vodka and tonic and introduced Baz to Mad Max, not the warmest of meetings, and told Baz to follow him over to meet Buster.

Introductions and other relations among musicians were an obscure art that Vic felt he'd never master—as much a challenge as the playing itself. Add to that the fact of color and the reality that these were Negro musicians making their only serious money in a white club to which only performing Negroes were admitted. Until

Tonto, the alto man, had invited him to Jake's, Vic was pretty sure they just let him play because they figured Eddie, the white man who owned the club, wanted them to.

Vic waited until Buster Cooper had paused in his warm-up and lowered his tenor, then said: "This is Baz, a trumpet man. He'd like to sit in if that's cool." Tonto was warming up facing the wall, blowing big, fat Cannonball phrases against it. Ernie Meeks was hitting tuning notes on the piano for the bass player, whom everybody called Honey Hush or just Hush. A trombone man Vic had never seen before was oiling his slide, and Baltimore smiled at Vic from behind his drum kit, then gave him a roll and a crash of the big Zildjian cymbal.

"Mercy," Buster said, shaking his head sadly. "I got this white boy alto hangin' 'round and now I got to have a ofay boy trumpet player?"

"Would Caldwell mind?" Vic asked. He didn't see Caldwell, Buster's trumpet man.

"Caldwell down with the flu," Buster said. "Whas your name again?"

"Baz," Baz said.

"Well, Baz, sit in on the ones you know, and if you in doubt, stay out. We'll see how you do." Vic should have heard Baz play more before he started this. Anybody could learn some hip warm-up doodles for the band room, so he didn't know if Baz could really play. But then, he wasn't so sure about himself, either.

"The Boop's gonna sing tonight," Buster said. "You boys can't play with her. She very fussy about who plays behind her." Betty Boop was a Negro singer Vic had wanted to hear. He and Baz nodded and opened their horn cases to warm up. As always, the only appropriate response to the building excitement of the crowd was to pretend they weren't there. Don't give them a piece of you. Just put out the music and be cool. Maybe they're payin', but we're playin'.

The first number was "The Preacher," the Horace Silver tune everybody was playing. It was funky blues, so Tonto had it all to himself. In fact, Buster said he didn't mind Vic's playing on the same stand with Tonto because their sounds were so distinct that it was like having two different instruments—Tonto's bold and sassy, and

Vic's thin, cool, almost like a trumpet. Vic joined in on the bridge and reprise of the chorus but didn't expect a solo and didn't get one. Baz used a mute at the mike on the eight bars they gave him—a strange choice on such a brassy number—but did all right.

Baz turned out to be one of those players who do well muted but stumble with an open bell. Then, in the midst of a nice muted sixteen bars Baz played on "I'll Take Romance," three tunes later, Vic thought of an answer for his own problem that had some of the force of revelation: He would check out the school's spare baritone sax and play it instead—in one stroke cutting the competition to maybe a tenth of what it was on alto, fitting into the Cooper combo without competing, and satisfying his father's worry about alto players—because there wasn't even a *record* yet of how long bari players lived. Instead of risking his voice in the full glare the alto invited, he'd rumble away in the cool shade, an octave below, where mistakes often sounded like intentional licks.

The trombone man took an indifferent sixteen bars. When Buster gave him a nod on "Romance," Vic was so relieved to have thought of the Baritone Escape that he played his alto unself-consciously, spontaneously, letting whatever came come, his swan song on a horn of doom—just barely noticing that Buster gave him another sixteen, then thirty-two more.

He had another revelation. Where had he learned all these great standards that kids didn't know today? Why, at Danny Sheehan's dance school—he and Val, Mrs. Messenger's Trained Performing Human Children, hoofing and goofing to the Tin Pan Alley Broadway melodies, one of the greatest outpourings of music the world had ever seen. And he was almost laughing through his embouchure as he brought it back down into the final bridge and chorus and just barely noticed that a beautiful black woman had come up near the stand, with a tall, wiry black man behind her, and was weaving, eyes closed, nodding with the music.

Buster called a break. Vic and Baz started putting their horns away, but Buster came over and said: "Boop says you can play. Ice don't like it, but when it comes to music Boop decides. Stay clear of Ice."

Vic felt the tension and split with Baz to the bar for the break.

He ordered a second and third vodka tonic, one to go, and Baz did the same. "Interesting," said Mad Max over the Mose Allison on the jukebox. "I can see you're going to have an interesting year." Vic just smiled and nodded, still high on his solo and Boop's invitation. "The Chinese have a curse," Max continued, "that goes, 'May you live in interesting times.'" Then he handed Vic a card with his name, address, and phone number. "Maxwell Gillette, Consultant." "What's his story?" Baz asked as they returned to the stand, and Vic shrugged.

Ice was a very dark-skinned man with straightened hair, a face like an African mask, and not an ounce of spare flesh. Prominent bones above the eyebrows and above his cheeks suggested the skull beneath. He wore small, round, wire-framed purplish-tinted glasses unlike anything Vic had ever seen. He generated a kind of smoldering power that occupied his own space and several others besides. None of the white customers went near him, though he stood directly in front of the band. As an almost ludicrous prop to make him look like an entertainer, part of the band, Buster had given him a wire bundle to hold that had been left behind by some amplified rock band and led nowhere.

Boop told Buster what she wanted to sing and then, before he could pass it on, turned to the band. "You know 'Something Cool'?" she asked, seeming to look at Vic, and everybody nodded. "In B-flat." Boop was not beautiful by ordinary white standards. She was short, probably five feet one even in high heels, and had full breasts, hips, and thighs, and her thin calves and ankles made her seem always a little uncertain on her feet—though she was probably high, too. Her hair was not straightened, was, in fact, cut fairly close to her head, and yet looked soft to the touch. She wore little makeup, her skin almost as dark as Ice's and with generous lips where his were thin. What made her beautiful, pulled it all together, was personality. Uncertain and vulnerable as she seemed from minute to minute, she projected something intangible that everybody felt and wanted, even through the dense field of Ice's hostility. Ernie gave them the first few chords. "Let's give these two young gentlemen a chance," Boop said. "Trumpet first, muted, then the alto."

Ernie played a very nice intro to the June Christy song and Boop sang, flattering the white singer by doing it much in her style, with some of the same vocal embellishments. Vic wondered what was going on. Was this white night with the Buster Cooper Combo— white trumpet, white sax, Negro singer doing a white vocal? Baz's eight bars were really pretty good—spare, teasing, almost lazy cool for a hot Indian summer Florida night, very much in character with the song. Vic had planned his solo, wanting to hit the ground running and dazzle Boop, but instead rushed it, spoiled it, fell all over himself, ruined the mood, and was grateful to finish on a note in the right key.

His face burned. He avoided eye contact with anybody, reaching for his drink and willing his heart to stop pounding. He wished a tidal wave would sweep the place away, erase any record or memory of this night. He knew everyone was looking at him, shaking their heads with disgust. Maybe a fire would break out and take their attention from him.

Instead, Ice said, in a low but metallic and very distinct voice: "So much for *white* music. Why don't you play something *real?*"

Buster closed his eyes. Baltimore coughed and pretended to drop a stick. Ernie tried to cover it over with some transitional chords.

Boop said something to Buster and he turned to them. "'Mean to Me,'" he said. "Same key."

Vic stepped off the stand, capped his mouthpiece, and laid his horn inside the open case behind. After some hesitation, Baz followed. They listened to Boop sing the song Billie Holiday had made her own, listened to the band's new life in response to Ice's challenge, heard the meaning behind the music in the invisible but almost palpable contact between Boop and Ice. She never looked at him, but everybody in the room felt it. Tonto picked up the anger and hurt, transforming it, as this music had always done, into joy and triumph. Buster took a more lyrical approach, asking the old questions that still had no answers but in the music, playing the best Vic had ever heard him play. Then Ernie began attacking the piano in great, sprawling chords, a furious syncopation unlike anything Vic had ever heard from him, crashing one atop another like waves, building long past any expectations and spending himself entirely until he nodded at Hush for an eight-bar bass solo, then gave it back to Boop for a last chorus.

Vic had been expecting trouble ever since Ice's remark. Nobody had ever done anything like that here. Surely some white drunk would insult him, push him, hit him with a bottle from behind like the guy who hit Bird. Ice didn't bother to watch his back. He kept his eyes locked on Boop, though she never once looked at him. And probably only the overwhelming performances, built on Ice's outrage, saved him from retaliation.

It was the custom to spend the second break on the beach. The audience was usually drunk enough not to begrudge them the extra time it took to smoke some grass in that fairly safe setting. He'd been invited before. Nobody withdrew the invitation now, and Baz wanted to follow them out, but Vic knew it was a mistake.

What little conversation there'd been stopped when he and Baz joined the group in the moonlight. The circle did not open for them. The smoke was acrid and sweet and now seemed forbidden to their kind. "What you want, Elvis?" Ice asked, still in a low voice but easily heard over the waves. "You steppin' all over your dick in there, boy."

"Let him be," Boop said.

It was not Ice's style to argue with a woman, so he didn't answer her.

Buster said: "He's all right."

Ice said: "No."

Vic and Baz walked away. Split the scene. They went inside and packed their horns, nodded at the drunken compliments and requests for "Night Train," had another quick drink each. Tonto came up and took Vic aside.

"You need to know about Ice. He's the real, cold evil, so don't ever lip him. Sheriff beat him for hustlin' white girls and he spit in the man's face. That's why his voice like that, husky, croaky-like; cop messed up his voice box choking him with a nightstick. He got so much hate in him it chased out whatever good might have been there before. If you gonna learn anything you gotta be alive."

"I played shitty," Vic said. "I'll never get it."

"You keep talking 'bout *it*," Tonto said. "We all just players, tryin' to get better."

"I mean talent, soul, what Bird had. Gotta suffer." Vic realized he'd drunk too much. He was full of self-pity.

Tonto laughed gently. "That's what God made Ice for. That why he made the horn so hard to play, life so hard to live. But you don't go 'round cryin' about it. Keep it inside for fuel, don't spill it sittin' at no bar. Think of it as a gift you can do somethin' with. That's soul. Ice's problem is he let anger about bad luck and trouble make him all hollow inside. But the outside's real scary. I just want to warn you. White folks think they safe from colored around here, and they usually are, but those rules don't apply to Ice. Stop takin' yourself so serious and take *him* serious. You want pain, he's the place. Good night, son. Whoo, that is some *reefer* Ice brought. Got me playin' daddy to some white boy. Later."

Vic and Baz left before the band came back for the last set. Baz was living above a funeral home in St. Pete. His dad was a former trumpet player and junkie who was night man at a cheap hotel downtown, but Baz didn't want to live with him. The funeral director gave him the apartment in exchange for Baz's working shifts answering the phone and helping with ambulance calls and pickups of the deceased on the odd shifts the full-time men didn't want to work. "We've got our *own* gage, man," Baz said and brought an already rolled joint from his bedroom. They smoked in silence at first, making the ritual noises and gestures that Vic was only just learning. Then Baz said: "That was the strangest tonight. Like the whole history of the thing was right *there*, and the future, too."

"I'm hip," Vic said. "Boy did I play shitty."

"Only that one time. You were cookin' until then."

There was a long pause.

"What would you do if you were high and on duty and somebody called?" Vic asked.

"I *am* on duty," Baz said.

Vic laughed as he drove home, imagining little bebop Baz saying to some woman: "Like I hate to be the one to bring you down, ma'am, but your old man is the deadest." Safe in his bedroom, he didn't want to hear any more music. He read in *Zhivago:* "He raised his head and from his vantage point absently glanced about the bare autumn landscape and the domes of the monastery. His snub-nosed face became contorted and he stretched out his neck. If a wolf cub had done this, everyone would have thought it was about to howl. The boy covered his face with his hands and burst into sobs. The wind bearing down on him lashed his hands and face with cold gusts of rain. A man in black with tightly fitting sleeves went up to the grave. This was Nickolai Nicholaievich Vedeniapin, the dead woman's brother and the uncle of the weeping boy; a former priest, he had been unfrocked at his own request. He went up to the boy and led him out of the graveyard."

Oh boy, Vic thought, sleepy and still high. "With love to lead the way, I've found more clouds of gray than any Russian play could guarantee." Now he understood the lyrics. This was going to be a bitch to read. A bitchevich. But it was Russia, so there must be Tatars. He leafed sleepily through the novel, finding no Tatars, and fell asleep.

He woke with his room full of men. His father and the three Riggins brothers: Lanny, Buddy, and Walker. They were giggling. It was still dark out. "You've heard of Bat Man," his father whispered. "This is Cat Man. Sleeps all day, only comes out at night. And he doesn't fight crime, he commits it."

The Riggins brothers sniggered. "I haven't seen him for four, five years," Lanny whispered.

"Well, I promised you a look. Let's not wake him."

"I'm awake," Vic said.

"Want to come fishin'?" Walker asked.

"No."

They left, still giggling like kids. He went back to sleep and woke about ten feeling great. His mother made him breakfast, and he scarfed bacon, scrambled eggs, toast, orange juice, and coffee with gusto. In the bathroom he threw up. Surprised, he tried to do it quietly.

Later, when he'd built up the courage to take out his horn again and practice, he found a note in his case: "Don't drink the orange juice, you moron!—A friend."

The Great Pretender

Home Room

Nothing.

Art

Down Beat

Woods-Quill-Shihab-Stein FOUR ALTOS—
Prestige. Rating *** Bird is dead, but the melody lingers on.
There is a distinct element of retro-gression inherent in this set.
The four altos project in the Bird manner, shouting ferociously
through the six tracks. The material is divided between
disguised standards and blowing session jumping-off riffs. The
four altos in unison is a fierce sound. And this, in a solo sense,
is a generally violent set. There is little harmonic interplay
among the saxes, but the soloists charge through, sweating out
their dues to Bird. Stein's playing is reasonably attractive.

Shihab and Woods are the most fluent, in the Bird tradition. Quill is wildly passionate, but his tone is strident. . . . I had the feeling I'd heard it all before. The frenzied statements are there, and capable musicianship, too. But it's Bird all over again, I would have preferred to hear one alto playing individualistically to four in such obvious echoes of the glorified past. (D.G.)

tangents By Don Gold
Charlie Parker died on March 12, 1955.

Those who worshipped him as a remarkably gifted musician and significant figurehead continue to pay homage to him, three years after his death. Today Bird is an image-provoking icon, an unseen force of the past.

And the number of blank faces forming the ranks of the Bird legion increases with individualism-stifling regularity. On decaying walls, at the end of letters to *Down Beat*, in whispered sounds, the two words appear: "Bird lives." Three years after his death, Parker's influence broadens to encompass a musical and socio-economic way of life.

For most of the prisoners of the myth, it is a one-way road to oblivion.

Bird is dead.

He spoke eloquently in a form of music that maturationally is in its infancy or early adolescence at best. Jazz is young, and Parker had the power of youth and the freshness only genuine invention can produce. But he spoke for himself, out of the bitterness and ecstasy of experience that belonged to him.

Today, a variety of jazzmen attempt to speak Bird's language, attempt to relive Bird's life. You hear them on LPs that flow into the market weekly. You hear them on every major instrument, writhing hopelessly in an effort to capture an adored past.

They won't make it. . . .

This kind of thinking is fallacious. And a detailed emulation of Bird can prove disastrous, in a musical and personal way, as many of Bird's associates can testify. . . .

Memories may linger, but the future must be faced.

Phys Ed

Field wet; girls using gym court; another damned movie about the future.

Study Hall

Hall pass. Library.

Doomed to a Smokeless Agony BRITISH ADDICTS GASP NOBLY THROUGH ANTITOBACCO EXPERIMENT depressed volunteers applaud listlessly as antismoking society's head, Lennox Johnson, warns waggishly against resuming foul habit   Poston, a comparative newcomer, plays the earnest drunk and is enormously funny in his wild battle against alcohol

In his second year as a pro, Fullback Jimmy Brown, 22, of the Cleveland Browns, has already had enough wild-eyed tributes   When Howard Hawks makes movies he likes to use unknown actresses and often comes up with startling results. . . . His latest and still unknown unknown is the girl resting above, Angie Dickinson

(a more unknown unknown than *Emily* Dickinson? Vic wondered)

Sometimes, to some perfectionists, the excitement of doing and living is too intense to bear. This can lead to tragedy, as shown in the brief, fiery life of Amedeo Modigliani   King Hussein of Jordan is the world's prime target for assassination Though Eliot is a master of serious, and often abstruse, poetry, he said, "I had more unadulterated pleasure out of *Old Possum's Book of Practical Cats* . . . than anything else I've ever written."

For years Smith's physical education department has been teaching posture to its freshmen   Singer Eartha Kitt had this privilege when she met Queen Elizabeth

He checked out *Genghis Khan: The Emperor of All Men:* "Seven hundred years ago, a man almost conquered the earth. He made himself master of half of the known world, and in-spired humankind with a fear that lasted for generations. In the course of his life he was given many names—the Mighty Manslayer, the Scourge of God, the Perfect Warrior, and the Master of Thrones and Crowns. He is better known to us as Genghis Khan."

Lunch

Emily Dickinson slipped him a note that read: "I broke up with Billy, but I have tickets to Homecoming at Gainesville. We'd have to sleep in the car unless we drove back that night and missed the parties. Does your dad still have that old fishing station wagon?" Was this a different girl from last year, or was this just an overnight dry fuck, and "sleeping" meant sleeping?

Jimmy Johanssen was crazy, Vic feared, beyond what it took to be a drummer. He wanted a car worse than anything, and his parents would not buy him one. At first it was just a joke when he pretended to have a car and drove it in the hallways, speed-shifting smoothly and burning rubber in the first three gears, down-shifting for the turns, doing good imitations of the sounds of Maserattis and Ferraris at Sebring. But Jimmy had been doing this for over a year now, more and more openly and seriously, and he was beginning to attract the wrong kind of attention.

Jimmy was tooling down C Wing to lunch, oblivious to Mickey Moran and the rats who awaited him in the middle corridor. Vic had to think fast. He made the noise of a siren and accelerated after Jimmy. Jimmy looked back in what appeared to be genuine fear. Vic waved him over and let the siren wind down.

Mick pointed to the goof, starting already to forget whatever meanness he'd had in mind and enjoy Vic's prank. You could read Mick Moran by his jaw, which mainly hung open. When he was bored, puzzled, or even amused, it hung down like the bucket of a steam shovel. On those rare occasions that it closed tight, trouble had already come to somebody. Vic had seen it close, and now, as Jimmy brought his imaginary vehicle to a full stop, he saw it open again.

Jimmy pulled over and Vic took his time, pretending to get out of the cruiser, walk up like Crump, and ask for Jimmy's license. Jimmy did have a license, if not a car, and he produced it meekly. Vic studied it, giving Mick time to take in his example of how to handle this for the other rats. Mick was laughing. So were a lot of other people.

"I'm going to let you go with a warning this time, Mr. Johanssen," Vic said finally. "With a vehicle capable of the speeds yours can deliver, you've got to be especially careful."

"It will never happen again," Jimmy promised and drove off slowly, seeming unaware of the laughter all along the wing—proud, in fact, of having a still unblemished driving record.

English

He told Mrs. Benoit that he'd be reading *Dr. Zhivago, A Portrait of the Artist as a Young Man, On the Road,* and *The Catcher in the Rye.* The first two he had to do for Miss Cook; the last two he'd already read during the summer. He spent the period reading about the Mongols and their Khan: "In the course of his campaigns within the Gobi, he had encountered the great wall and considered attentively this rampart of brick and stone with its towers over the gates and its impressive summit upon which six horsemen could gallop abreast."

Music Theory

Bust ass. Miss Cook showing no mercy. She says the very least a serious musician must have is total command of his instrument and a thorough knowledge of music theory. Quotes Mingus and Diz. Now let's begin. Using the notebook for the first time. Music is mathematical. Man, it better *not* be. Damn, slow down!

Band

Mr. Branthooven announced the Fall Concert, the repertoire including the band's accompaniment of an alto saxophone solo by Victor Messenger on a piece called "Beautiful Colorado." Vic was surprised. They'd discussed it tentatively last year and he knew the piece, a syrupy thing requiring technical virtuosity and not an iota of soul and ending on a special fingering of A above high C. OK, he said, thank you, and they began working on it and the other concert numbers.

After band Baz told him Louis Armstrong was going to play the Manhattan Casino. They'd booked him at the Coliseum, but when he found out Negroes couldn't attend, he cut a new deal. Solid. Let's fall by. But how do *we* get in? Would they set aside Thursday for whites?

Home

Practiced "Beautiful Colorado." Watched TV with Mom and Dad. Val came through, looking mysterious, and he remembered he no longer drank orange juice. He put on the earphones at bedtime and listened again to Quill's solo on "The Ballad of Tappan Zee." Jesus, that wasn't Birdcalls, imitations. That was It. And, to paraphrase Satch, if you can't already recognize It, Don Gold, then don't bother.

Basin Street Blues

Two-Two Street buzzed like a swarm of bees—
in this case following not the queen but the king to the Manhattan
Casino and busying itself with eager efforts to make him happy and
enjoy his goodwill, his music. Baz was afraid to risk his car—liber-
alism ending in his case where his rusted 1948 Plymouth began—
so the two white boy hipsters had literally buzzed down to Frenchtown on Vic's new/old Crusaire scooter, locking its fork under a fire
escape in the alley behind and emerging onto the street trying to
look as though they not only had arrived in a groovy short but were
also expected, even welcomed.

Such was not the case. The line ran from the second-floor ballroom down the stairs and along the street—and that was for those
already holding tickets. Reactions to the only two whites in Frenchtown that night were of two types: (1) The leper treatment. They were
present but one did not look at them, for to do so would raise questions that had no answers. (2) The invisible man approach. They

were not present, and if one avoided walking through the space they seemed to occupy, it was only by accident. The guy taking tickets was of the second school. Vic held out their tickets and he ignored them, reaching past to accept tickets from people behind them in line. Vic laid the tickets down, but the man still refused to see them. Maybe they lay there unclaimed through the night. Nor did the man see Vic and Baz as they walked past him finally in frustration to join the crowd on the dance floor.

They joined nothing, really. Paths opened for them where they went, but as if by accident. At one point a man seemed to approach, his hand open in greeting, but then he reached past Vic's shoulder to slip skin to a friend behind. The band was tuning up behind the stage. Men were strutting. Women were flirting, vamping, sassing. The air was thick with perfume, cologne, and smoke, both legal and illegal. Vic had never felt so isolated. This is it, he thought; the real, red-hot center of it. Storyville, the delta blues, upriver migrations, Memphis, Kansas City, St. Louis, Chicago, Harlem— the moochers, vipers, hipsters—all of it embodied in the man whose trumpet he heard backstage. And Vic was here, and he was invisible. If he screamed, they wouldn't hear him.

He motioned to Baz and headed for the stage. At least they could take this advantage of their leper status. Baz took out a moogle, as it was appropriate to call it there that night, and they smoked it seemingly unnoticed. "I see you, man," Baz said, goofing. "Do you see me?"

"I *see* you," Vic said, "but I'm not sure I can *dig* you. What if the kids at school could see us now?"

"At least that would be somebody who could," Baz said. "Maybe we don't exist any more. Maybe we're gone."

"We're real gone tonight," Vic agreed.

They stood directly below the bandstand, but when Armstrong came out with his musicians, peered through the lights, shaded his eyes to see the crowd and pretend surprise, even exchanging greetings with some, he didn't see them either.

But he played, and for that set, and the next, Vic didn't mind being invisible. Here was what the records couldn't capture, the real breath, the pulse, the sweated sweetness. Vic realized, with the real Armstrong on a real stage above him, that he'd never been entirely sure such people existed, that he'd held without even knowing it some childish notion that the music had been conjured, maybe like the Huns of Goth legend, from a union of banished spirits and sand, and that the people he played with in school and local clubs were just a low order of the priesthood that worshipped them by imitation. Or, like the South Pacific cargo cults he'd read about, they worshipped the exterior of the plane or the goods fallen from the sky without ever understanding the objects' original purpose. Seeing Armstrong—veins bulging at his temples, eyes popped and red-rimmed with the effort of playing, sweat rolling in the spotlight—seemed no less amazing than if suddenly Christ should appear, or Attila.

Baz went away and returned with four cold beers. "I ran into Buster," he said. "He was real nice, and pretty high. He offered to get 'em and I got two extras." But he'd forgotten to get them opened and they didn't have a church key, so they stood for a long time just holding the four warming beers, a minor cargo cult unto themselves, breathing the smoke, taking in the music, until a man they didn't know stepped up and grabbed the beers and popped all four with his own key, saying "Damn!" to suggest the frustration of his inability to ignore their stupid plight any longer. They thanked him, and he said, "Sheeeit." They drank them fast, for their thirst and for the buzz. Vic had seldom felt worse than tonight, and never better.

On the next break they crowded into the men's room and in their turns urinated without incident, though Vic had a mild attack of shy bladder and heard some grumbling behind him. "At least they didn't try to *piss* through us," Baz said when they were back on the floor.

They ran into Buster, with Tonto. To Vic's surprise, they were cautiously friendly. "Sorry about the other night," Buster said. They made small talk.

Vic said, "I guess we're safe here."

Tonto, with a chance finally to live up to his name, said, "What's this *we* shit, white man?" And they cracked up.

Vic felt a change and looked around. Since they'd been talking with Buster and Tonto, people had begun to admit their existence. Baz felt it too and tried it at the bar, and came back with four more cold beers, all opened, and change.

Tonto took Vic aside. "You and I got to have a talk," Tonto said. He was high on something but serious. "About your playin'."

Vic felt a chill, and his face must have shown it. Now Tonto was looking straight at him, probably for the first time. "You got talent," he said. "But you need to get some things straight. What I'm sayin' is you need to have somebody with experience teach you a philosophical approach. Dig?"

Vic nodded. He didn't know exactly what Tonto was describing, but he wanted it.

"Come on," Buster said. "We'll take you back to meet the man."

Backstage, Armstrong seemed too real. His sidemen were off somewhere doing what musicians do on breaks. The room was crowded but hushed, the mood one of reverence. Satch was seated in a large chair, like a throne, his black face serious, shining with sweat. He reminded Vic of some ancient god—Moloch, maybe, who ate children. On his right knee was a good-looking blonde white girl in a tight, short, low-necked green dress. On his left knee, wearing red lipstick and nails, a long, waved, auburn wig, and a similar red dress, sat Betty Boop. Ice stood in a corner, his eyes averted, but Armstrong was looking straight at them, and so was Boop, without apparent recognition.

"These boys came down to meet you," Buster said.

Armstrong let a few beats go by. "You boys a long way from home," he said finally. Then he asked: "Are you musicians?"

"No," Vic said, obeying his first instinct. Baz followed his lead and shook his head.

Boop whispered into Armstrong's ear, and slowly he smiled. "Now you told me a lie," he said. "Why you want to lie about that?" They were being judged, and whatever they said, they'd be condemned.

"We're not any good," Vic said. Somehow it seemed urgent that he make that clear.

"That ain't what I heard," Satch said. He let another bar go by. "I hope you ain't a couple of them beboppers, them poor boys with they flatted fifths. Are you boys beboppers?"

Vic wondered how he'd gotten to be the spokesman for his contemporaries, his race, jazz after World War II. Baz was sitting this one out. No help there.

Finally Vic said: "We hope to go beyond that, build on that and what you've done."

Satch laughed, and so did the others. It seemed good-natured and Vic accepted it as his dues for being young and white and saying something as pretentious as he'd just said. He laughed with them.

"Go beyond that," Satch repeated, and that set him off laughing again.

Finally the laughter subsided.

"Yeah," Satch said, "you boys a long, *long* way from home."

In the Mood

On one of the first cool nights of that autumn of
1958, a cotillion was held at the Bartlett Park Youth Center for young
people ages thirteen and fourteen to learn dancing and social skills.
The basketball hoops were cranked on winches ceilingward, and the
gym mats, standing horse, balance beam, parallel bars, and high
bar were removed or pushed to the side and draped with canvas. All
but the first three rows of the bleachers, accordion-like in design,
were pushed backward. Boys sat on one side, girls on the other.
The dance took place under the iron rule of a tiny, painted woman
of some fifty years named Honoria (the kids pronounced it to rhyme
with *gonorrhea*) Velasquez and her partner, who wore a tuxedo,
Vaselined hair, and a pencil-thin moustache, and was known only
as Mr. Robert.

Nothing could remove the smell of sweat from this space, but then
the kids were sweating, too, mainly from anxiety, and a trickle could
be noticed now and then down Mr. Robert's temple. Miss Honoria

Velasquez did not sweat—had, in fact, a reptilian sort of metabolism. Because she ran the show and welcomed heat, there was no cross ventilation. She stood beneath her amazing, lacquered hair, cool as some glazed ceramic lamp base, while the kids sweated, Mr. Robert sweated, and, behind them on the bandstand, Benny Greene and the Blue Notes sweated. At the end of this magic, if somewhat sultry, evening, each of the Blue Notes would pocket twenty-five dollars. Benny, a trumpet player, was two years out of high school. Friends of his from the other high school played bass and tenor sax. Vic played alto. Jimmy Johanssen was on drums, Dale Cleaver on trombone, and Benny's mom played piano.

Vic didn't listen to Miss Velasquez's welcoming and warning speech. They had a list of arrangements, and "In the Mood" sat ready on his cardboard music stand, the one with Benny's and the band's names on the front in paint and sparkle dust. And besides, he'd heard it all before, when he was one of the sweaty kids down there on the first three rows of the bleachers. They'd actually had to rehearse this gig because Miss Velasquez and Mr. Robert would demonstrate and teach not only the fox-trot but the rumba, tango, mambo, the cha-cha-cha, and the jitterbug.

But first the kids must learn the etiquette of the ballroom. Miss Velasquez had a stern and strident voice, and a microphone to amplify it further. The kids fidgeted as she spoke, listening only for the change of pitch that would signal the end of the speech—they had all been warned by earlier cotillioners—and the permission to approach their partners. Most of the boys had come in new leather shoes at their parents' insistence, though they'd also been warned that shoes must be removed to protect the court's polished wooden surface. So they were uncertain of their purchase on that slick varnish, and many were experimenting with traction as Miss Velasquez spoke. She saw a boy remove his socks and reprimanded him sternly, holding up the whole show until he'd put them back on.

And most of the boys had also been warned by veterans of this dance to wear jockstraps against the possibility of the unplanned adolescent erection, because, after all, despite anything Miss Velasquez might say—which all of them, including Mr. Robert, were ignoring—the whole point of this evening was to tear across the floor first and find a girl—most boys had already picked their girl, squinting in the strange gym light—who (1) had breasts and (2) was from a different junior high school. To succeed in this was teen heaven. To fail was to spend a hellish four or five minutes with your arms just barely around one of the Tomboys or Stick Figures or Fatsos you'd spent your whole life trying to avoid.

Vic could hear that time approaching. There were still times, lots of times, when he wished he'd worn his trusty slow-dance jock, when, daydreaming through one of his crib classes or even walking the halls, thinking about harem houris, the fabled Levantine whores, dusky jazz singers like Boop, or even the mysteries Emily Dickinson now claimed, he'd spring the embarrassing boner and have to sit it out where he was, forcing himself to think instead of being decapitated by a scimitar or run over by a train or a herd of wild horses to tame his wild organ. Of course this never happened in gym class, where he was already wearing a jockstrap.

Miss Velasquez was not unaware of her enormous power at this point. She milked the moment, made them sweat. Then she gave the signal. "Gentlemen," she began, and the boys—many of them already crouched in sprinter's stance—took off. They slipped. They fell. They all seemed to be heading—a convergence of libido—toward one place. Then Vic saw her, as if suddenly lighted by a baby spot. She was tall for her age and blonde. She had a pleasant face and a somewhat bashful smile at being the target of this volley of Cupid's arrows. She was wearing a skirt and dressy sweater. She had large breasts.

It wasn't clear right away who had claimed her in the confusion caused by (1) a boy being knocked unconscious in his fall to the court, and (2) Miss Velasquez noticing that the chosen girl was chewing gum and demanding that she remove it before the dance could begin. The girl laughed good-naturedly and took it out, and Vic wondered all that evening where she'd put it. It simply disappeared. And she, the object of all this desire, spent the evening in the arms of one lucky (and shorter) boy after another—the boy most often with his cheek against her breasts and his eyes closed like a nervous dog whose ears are being scratched for the first time. For much of the evening her eyes were on the bandstand.

They fox-trotted. They rumbaed. They sweated. They mamboed, cha-cha-chaed, jitterbugged, tried to tango, and even, once, bunny-hopped because Miss Velasquez tried to use it as a basis for teaching the conga and samba. But the band hadn't rehearsed a conga or samba, although they replayed their mambo arrangement faster, then slower. In any case, the kids by now were having so much fun being horny and confused that they were ungovernable, even by Miss Velasquez. She ordered them back to the bleachers, then gave Benny the signal for "Good Night Sweetheart," and a second boy was knocked unconscious in the rush. The blonde girl took it all rather gracefully. She was chewing the gum again, but Miss Velasquez knew when to quit.

The girl was waiting outside. She walked up to Vic and he stopped to let the other grinning band members walk past. "Hi," she said, chewing the gum provocatively. "You got a car?"

How much difference was there in their ages? Four years? If they were in their thirties, that would mean nothing. In the ancient world, men his age were seasoned warriors and women her age were mothers, wives, concubines, slaves. If he were a warrior in the great Ordu, the Golden Horde, he could claim her among the spoils of battle. She could be a blonde Slav or a Circassian—Vic didn't know exactly what a Circassian was, but they were in all the books when the writer needed a blonde, just as blacks were always Nubians—whom he could drag off to his yurt.

Except that *she* was asking *him*, and waiting for an answer. Jimmy Johanssen made a weird engine-revving noise from the dark parking lot, and he heard some laughter. She was making it so easy, which was how it had to be for him. He'd always known that he was no smoothie, no seducer. This attraction some women felt to musicians was really his only hand to play, and why shouldn't he? Four years ago he had been one of these horny kids, jockstrap-girded and swollen with lust. There had probably been a girl like this there—mature already and maybe also doomed to be old at twenty—and she'd probably gone off with the cute guy in the band. Now he was the cute guy in the band, and how long would *his* youth last? "Sure," he said. "I got a car."

She liked the car a lot. He drove to Lake Maggiore, where his dad sometimes fished for bass. He parked in a dark spot near the water, and she moved over to him as easily as if Miss Velasquez had just ordered it. She kissed with her mouth open, too open, and when he pulled up her sweater she helped him. It was no sooner off than she was climbing into the backseat, and by the time he'd followed her, she'd taken off her bra and was working on her skirt. She smelled of Chiclets, a perfume that suggested orange blossoms a little too strongly, and, just a little, of sweat.

He was clumsy, but she helped him. She produced a rubber—perhaps from the same secret place the gum had disappeared to—and put it on him. It was over quickly, but he felt her move in three or four quick turns beneath him and heard her little grunts of pleasure. Afterward, she gave him a few little kisses on his face and let him hold her awhile before complaining that the armrest was hurting her neck. It was the first thing she'd said since outside the gym. He thought it was interesting that she hadn't been a virgin while he had, and he was very glad he wasn't any more, with so little confusion, but there was nobody he could tell about it.

That night in bed he read *The March of the Barbarians:* "When you are Khan, we will obey you. We shall stand in the front of battle against your foes. When we take captive beautiful girls, we will give the best of them to you."

Rock Around the Clock

Home Room

The principal let an AV dork named Tommy Haney pretend to be a rock DJ on the school PA system. He'd rigged a turntable and even had some stupid promo jingles for something called "Tiger Radio." There was only time to play the one Bill Haley song, but Vic saw it as an ominous sign.

Art

Down Beat

Johnny Richards THE RITES OF DIABLO Personnel: Studio band, including Gene Quill, alto. . . . Throughout this work, Richards has tried to weld the Bantu rhythms to American jazz, using material from the folk music of Cuba. . . . soloists including Powell, Quill, Collins, Copeland. . . . and the

Lambert singers perform creatively within Richards'
format   SONNY STITT. . . . plays Charlie Parker's style with
such personal conviction and such emotional sureness and
without any hint of slickness, popularization, or stylistic
immaturity. . . . Stitt worked on the basic conception first, and
grasped it. Then he worked on the virtuosity and technique to
fill out and elaborate it. How many others tried it the other way
and failed?   To the Editor: In a recent newspaper interview,
disc jockey Alan Freed was asked if rock and roll was music.
His reply was, "I certainly hope so! After all, it's the only
American music that we can call our own. . . ." After reading
this I suddenly became violently ill
    To the Editor: I am a teenager and dislike being classed into
the group that limits its scope of musical appreciation to such
classical works of "art" as "Purple People Eater"
    At press time, as plans began to jell for the affair, the Albam
band was set to include jazzmen from an available pool,
including Ernie Royal, Bernie Glow, Art Farmer, Nick Travis,
Gene Quill, Al Cohn, Zoot Sims, Pepper Adams   ART
PEPPER MEETS THE RHYTHM SECTION Red Garland, piano;
Paul Chambers, bass; Philly Joe Jones, drums. . . . This
memorable meeting deserves a favored place in anybody's
collection   Phil Woods WARM WOODS. . . . When Woods is
less Bird and more himself, he speaks with authoritative
originality   Berklee School JAZZ IN THE CLASSROOM—
Berklee Records   Dick Clark, a well-groomed adult with a
teenage mentality, sells chewing gum to the youth of
America   Jean Thielmans TIME OUT FOR TOOTS . . .
Thielmans, harmonica and guitar. . . . is the 36-year-old
Belgian (now a U.S. citizen) who has been guitarist (with
occasional harmonica solos) with the George Shearing quintet
since late 1952. . . . many refuse to accept the harmonica as
anything but a toy   Juilliard Heads East. . . . resident
student orchestra left for a tour of Europe   ALTO SAX—NEW
STAR La Porta (25), Adderley (25), McLean (25), Mariano (20),
Quill (20)   Recently, Cole Porter reached 65. And, as they

said in the old days of radio continuity, it is "a milestone in music." For along with Irving Berlin (70), Oscar Hammerstein (63), Richard Rodgers (56), and Harold Arlen (53), he represents the living old guard that has made "show music" a brilliant thread in American popular music   Gene Quill THREE BONES AND A QUILL. . . . Quill carries the strident voice in the group and continues to retain his rights to the title Angry Young Man of the Saxophone   When this magazine reported on Shelly Manne's high fidelity system (*Down Beat*, June 27, 1957) he was quoted as saying, "When I go into a hi-fi store and they play music for me on those super-duper rigs, I really don't enjoy it. I don't *hear* the music that way . . . and I don't feel I need that kind of equipment. . . . Alert to advances in the field of sound reproduction, however, Shelly now feels that it is practicable to make the switch to stereo   JAZZ CAN BE TAUGHT, by Lawrence Berk, Executive Director, Berklee School of Music   STAN FREBERG. . . . ("tuned" sheep, with bells around their necks, playing *Lullaby of Birdland*)   *Cross Section* Art Pepper "Living without love is like not living at all"

At the bell, Emily Dickinson slipped him a note that read: "Are you going to Homecoming with me or not?"

Phys Ed

The dread day they had to run a mile. Vic barely made it, coughing, wondering about cigarettes. Six kids collapsed along the way, another in the shower.

Study Hall

Hall pass. Library.
The roles of swamp angels are taken by Emmett Kelly, the renowned clown, Tony Galento, the famous boxer, Burl Ives, once a ballad singer, and Sammy Renick, former jockey. Gypsy

Rose Lee   Hollywood likes to think of Actress Debbie Reynolds and Singer Eddie Fisher as its ideal couple

I Dreamed I Was Made Over In My Maidenform Bra   Vice President Nixon leaves the trampoline to the younger members of the family   RCA VICTOR ANNOUNCES STEREO SOUND ON RECORDS   In New York race, Harriman and Rockefeller, civic-minded heirs of "robber barons"

Until now, no smoke has ever tasted as vividly fresh, as downright pleasurable as the first flavorful puff at breakfast. Why? Because then, rested taste buds actually bloom, are at their peak of taste-sensitivity. Now you can keep them that way, smoke after smoke, with Smith Brothers new Smokers Drops   Thirty million dollar Desilu gamble: Arnaz and Ball take over as tycoons   THINKING OF CAREER, Elvis ponders question: "What would you do if the rock 'n' roll fad died out?" His reply: "Why, I'd just starve to death."   Wash and Wear   Man is not made for defeat. Man can be destroyed, but not defeated   Can Colleges Handle 60s Crowding?   ONLY VICEROY HAS A THINKING MAN'S FILTER   Jackie Gleason briefly wears a moustache   De Gaulle goes to work on his big problem, Algeria   in Guatemala jungle scientists uncover great 1,000-year-old metropolis   Five generations of Rin Tin Tin   AT HIS WINDOW overlooking Second Avenue, painter Larry Rivers warms up on the saxophone while waiting for friends to arrive for the weekly jam session   WIDER GRILLE is one of the minor changes made on the hugely successful American Motors Rambler   Kennedy hopes for a landslide win   Pasternak is an eminent poet who has translated Shakespeare and Goethe into Russian   Georges Simenon has written 400 novels . . . and most were written in only 11 days   Members of the class of 1959 in Little Rock and Virginia get patchwork schooling or none   STAR STUDENT at Granby . . . says, "If we had a choice I think even the colored people would rather be alone."   The intensity of competition, moreover, has produced perfection in every artifice of mimicry and illusion. Since a single flaw means sudden death, survival of the fittest means survival of the craftiest, slyest, and most artful in the murmurous, implacable domain   "HULA HOOP" is sung by Steve Allen, here rehearsing his TV show   General MacArthur did not seem to share the President's sense of humor   See it now at your Edsel Dealer. Ten history-making new models!   BERLIN GIRDS FOR BLOCKADE   Relief is just a swallow away

Check out *Tamerlane: The Earth Shaker*.

Lunch

Sloppy Joes, whole-kernel corn, coleslaw, vanilla pudding. Vic skipped the smoke break, sitting in the backseat of the Olds pretending to be looking for a paper, half an erection, thinking about the blonde and hoping to catch her smell again there where it had happened.

English

Mrs. Benoit said they would all be required to learn and recite Chaucer's prologue to *The Canterbury Tales*. Vic took off his shades and winked, and she said, "*Every*body. No exceptions." When Shellie Glass asked what use it would be to them in later life, she said: "Maybe none. Maybe it will rattle in your empty heads like a pea in a gourd. Maybe it will haunt you like a tune you can't get out of your mind, and you'll find it on your tongue as you build houses or vacuum carpets or sell hardware. Maybe someone will make you memorize something else you don't think is of practical use—the armed forces are good at that—and you'll think, I already did Chaucer. How hard could this be? Maybe someday you'll be in a bad spot and need a prayer, and not be able to think of one. In a foxhole, a hospital bed, an overturned car. And you'll find yourself saying, 'When that Aprill' and so on. Maybe you'll just remember it fifty years from now and smile." Mrs. Benoit was in some mood that day.

He read in *Tamerlane*: "Not the son of a king, as Alexander was, or the heir of a chieftain, like Genghis Khan. The victorious Alexander had at the outset his people, the Macedonians, and Genghis Khan had his Mongols. But Tamerlane gathered together a people."

Music Theory

God, slow down, lady!

Band

Rehearsal for concert, most of it on "Beautiful Colorado."

Home

Practice "Beautiful Colorado."
Read: "The chronicle tells us of Timur's bride that her beauty was like the young moon, and her body graceful as the young cypress. She must have been about fifteen years of age, because she had been allowed to ride to the hunts with her father."

Hot Nuts

Florida won the game, beating arch rival Florida State by seventeen points in a game some called the world's second-largest outdoor cocktail party—the first being Florida-Georgia in the Gator Bowl. Vic Messenger and Emily Dickinson (no relation) had come to town early enough to get a parking place behind the Delt house, which had a reputation for the best parties. Vic had drunk a half-pint of rum in the sun watching the game or he wouldn't have gone near the place afterward, but Emily pleaded that her friends would be there, and he agreed, with the notion that he would go as an observer and social critic.

Inside, the fraternity house resembled an insane asylum from an earlier century, some literal Bedlam. Young people lurched from room to room, inebriate eyes half closed, shrieking "Goooo *Gat*ors!" Boys pawed girls and other boys in an infantile way. Girls hung on their boyfriends, on one another, kissing, grooming, sometimes just hanging on so as not to fall and be trampled on the floor. One girl was dragged through the living room with her hands locked onto her boyfriend's belt. He seemed oblivious to the extra weight.

Emily Dickinson, a small person, was also, it turned out, a mean drunk. She'd had several rum-laced Cokes toward the end of the game and had gone quickly through the giddy phase during their parking lot passage with the exultant exiting crowd. She'd become maudlin on their half-mile walk to fraternity row, calling Vic a "good ole shit" and holding his arm to shed tears briefly on his shirt-sleeve. He'd offered her the last of his drink before the Delt house, misjudging her hummingbird metabolism, and she now was pushing him before her into huge, drunken frat boys, saying "Move it or lose it" and "Kick ass, Victor!" Vic had taken off his shades because he didn't want to be conspicuous here, but Emily wasn't making it easy. He was, in fact, trying to talk his way out of a fight with a very large sober Gator, fresh from the locker-room shower—Emily still pushing him against the brute, saying, "Punch 'im, knock his block off"—when someone saved him by announcing Super Nigger.

From one surrealism to another. Everybody crowded toward the door to the patio, including the lineman whose block Emily had wanted knocked off. They were among the last to make it through, and Emily climbed Vic like a drunken monkey to look over the crowd at the Negro man dressed only in cut-off jeans who was just then driving a spike through a fold of skin on his forearm with a hammer. His spiky hair seemed caked with mud. He had already pierced both cheeks with large safety pins.

When the applause died down, Super Nigger broke several empty whiskey bottles on the stage, then reduced them further with the hammer to razor-edged shards. He climbed atop the piano and danced a bit. Someone Vic couldn't see was playing the tom-tom on a drum kit at stage left. The crowd chanted "Super Nigger, Super Nigger." The tom-tom changed to a snare drum roll, building. Then, as Vic looked away, the man jumped. Vic heard Emily yell "Oh, God," felt her legs and arms tighten ambiguously on him, heard the roar of approval and applause. When he looked back, the man was laughing, dancing on the broken glass, skin pierced by nails and pins.

Later he'd get a check, but now people were throwing money,

mostly coins. When the rain of coins slowed and almost halted, the man picked up a piece of glass and began to chew it. Now there were wadded bills pelting the stage, and he smiled to show his pleasure, and the blood in his mouth.

"Fuck this," Vic said, but they could not get out. For a while they surged with the mob on the patio, in one direction or another, for no apparent reason. Emily had passed out and he was carrying her piggyback, only the crowd holding her upper body close to him because his arms were locked around her legs. Apparently what held them all trapped was that a rumor had gotten out about the Chocolate Drops playing, and everyone from the other parties was trying to get in. Vic learned this through shouts, screams, curses, and strangled mutterings. Apparently the force outside was greater than the resistance inside, so Vic and the unconscious Emily found themselves, through a quirk of this human tide, below the bandstand. He looked up and saw Buster Cooper. Buster saw him. Vic thought: Seldom have two people been less prepared to explain their presence to each other.

Then the Drops hit "Annie Had a Baby" and the whole packed mob of middle-class white adolescents began—because they were now physically locked together—to bounce. Buster played a different style of tenor here—the Honker, Bar Wailer Rhythm and Blues-style sax with a fat lower register sound, sometimes given a burr vibrato with the tongue, and lots of held and repeated high notes that for even the dimmest in the crowd made it clear that somebody was really cookin'. At its worst, it was the kind of cheap trick Vic himself was often called upon to do with Benny Greene and the Blue Notes, when the wedding or bar mitzvah crowd had thinned to the serious partiers and they wanted some safe soul. At its best, it was the Chocolate Drops, who all had other gigs and groups, like Buster, but who made the most money doing this for rich white kids.

They played "Take Out Some 'Surance," "Slippin and A'slidin'," "C.C. Rider," and, of course, "Hot Nuts." They had a good male singer. White kids were screaming approval from as far away as the alley behind and the lawn of the frat house across the street. The band's sound system carried even farther. White kids were passing out, urinating, vomiting as they stood locked together by black music. It was so bad it was almost good, had gone so far that it had almost made the loop back. Vic began to think he could weather it. Then, a frat man he didn't know recognized him—from playing with Buster at the Cypress Room, Vic guessed—and began, between numbers, to shout: "White sax, white sax, white sax!"

It was crazy. The bandleader, who was also the piano man, tried to read the situation as the crowd squeezed Vic and Emily through it, above it, and onto the stage. The bandleader forced a smile. Buster did too. The bass man helped Vic find a comfortable place on the stand for Emily Dickinson to sleep it off.

Buster pulled down the choke on his neck strap, took it off with the horn over his head, and handed the whole package to Vic. Vic didn't take it. "I don't play tenor," he said into the mike. "I'm not—"

"Play that horn, motherfucker!" someone screamed. Buster was still holding it out.

"How about 'Work Song'?" Vic asked the leader, choosing a Nat Adderley composition.

"That ain't what they come to hear," he said.

"Fuck 'em," Vic said.

"Easy for you to say," the leader said.

"Play the goddamn horn," someone else bellowed.

"*Not* so easy," Vic said. He took Buster's tenor and played a few experimental notes, tasting Buster's gin, tobacco, his salty mouth. He took off the mouthpiece and blew backward through it to clear the spit, then rubbed the reed gently across his pants leg to clear it of that residual moisture. He put it back on and tuned with the piano. He asked for a key and then made sure he could find the main riff notes on the B-flat tenor.

"Play the horn, you son of a bitch," somebody yelled, and Buster smiled for the first time.

"How's it feel?" he asked, and Vic knew a little bit of the answer. He got it together with the trumpet and trombone that they'd all play the riff together, no harmony the first time, and the trumpet would have the first solo. There were lyrics to it, too, and the singer knew them. It was a tune that began on a beat from the rhythm section, like the fall of a hammer on a chain gang. The leader counted one, two, three, four, and they hit it together:

BANG   Breakin' up big rocks on uh chain gang
BANG   Breakin' rocks an' servin' my time.
BANG BANG   Breakin' rocks ou' chere on the
    chain gang
BANG   'Cause I been convicted o' crime
BANG BANG   Hol' it steady right there while I hit it
BANG   There! I reckon that oughta git it
BANG   Been workin' an' workin'
BANG   But I still got so terrible long to go!

The crowd sensed that they were not exactly getting the nigger music they'd paid (or not paid) for, but it was close enough, and Vic's honky solo sounded just about right for a white kid, so they let the rest go. Vic experienced a kind of surrender in which the important part of him had retreated behind the other part that was doing what the crowd demanded, giving just enough signals for the remote parts to keep working while he watched from there. Emily was even farther removed, sleeping peacefully behind the guitar amp/speaker.

When the number was over, the applause was fairly enthusiastic. The mob had, after all, gotten its way. Vic gave the tenor back to Buster. "Sorry," he said.

Buster waved him off. "Ain't your fault," he said. Buster left the stage and began packing his horn.

The Chocolate Drops' leader said, "Buster, what you doin', man?" Buster didn't answer.

Without thinking, Vic bent to the sax mike and said: "You know, you people are a fucking disgrace."

After a few beats someone yelled, "Right. You goddamn right we are!"

"You make me ashamed to be white, to be a human being," Vic said, and he could hear it reverberating out across the campus.

"Yeaaah!" someone screamed. "We're animals!" And the crowd began chanting the word. They liked what Vic had said. They thought he'd said it in the spirit of brotherly dissipation, as a compliment. Apparently nobody could imagine that he'd say it any other way.

The bandleader relaxed when the cheers came up from those proud, degraded Gators who were still conscious. "You better quit," he said to Vic. "While you still ahead."

Buster helped him get Emily over his shoulder, and together they took the back way out, Vic carrying Emily, Buster his sax. "You can come back to town with us," Vic said.

"It's OK," Buster said. "I know some people here."

He walked away, across the well-tended, bottle-littered campus, toward his friends, growing smaller as Vic watched.

Emily moved, coughed, moaned. He bent and helped her stand. At least she hadn't thrown up. She threw up. They made their uncertain way back to the car. Emily had brought a picnic lunch, but it was growing dark now and it would be supper instead, eaten by Vic alone—surprised he was hungry, feeling almost sober, purged somehow—scarfing fried chicken on the tailgate of his dad's old rusty, green, Chevy fishing wagon. Emily moaned inside for a while, but even her hangover passed with hummingbird rapidity, and soon she was only remorseful, swearing to Vic that she would never drink again.

They sat in the car, listening to the parties all around them. Vic thought about Buster walking, still walking, maybe walking all the way back to St. Pete and beyond to Frenchtown.

"I was going to surprise you with something," Emily said. "With my mouth. I don't get pregnant . . . You know?"

He thought he did.

"But I don't feel very well," she said.

"That's OK," he said. He didn't either. Maybe Buster was with his friends, laughing about all this, having a big party.

After a while, Emily asked, "What were we doing on the bandstand?"

"I don't think I can explain it," Vic said.

He put his arm out and she leaned against him.

After a while, Emily said "I'm feeling better now. Want your surprise?"

"That's OK," Vic said. He still had the image of Buster walking with his sax case across the campus, getting smaller.

After a while, Emily surprised him.

Beautiful Colorado

His father feared the Boca Chica parking lot and the hubcap thieves he claimed lived there full time, "disguised as grease spots." He'd gone twice before to hear Vic play and had both times lost all four Fiesta spinner hubcaps on the big 1954 Oldsmobile 98 that was his special pride. It was the first "hardtop convertible" made in Detroit and had the first car air conditioner anyone had seen, with long ducts rising from the rear panel. It was dark and light green and almost too long for the garage, but he kept it there for safety's sake. And it seemed safe anywhere else in town but the high school parking lot.

His dad liked to have the first of anything new. They had a TV set a year before there was anything broadcast close enough to see on it. It had set there in the living room like a very dirty aquarium or the screen Big Brother used in *1984*. When the first station went on the air, it offered only four hours of programming a day. There were two newscasts, some cartoons, films of people singing Hit Parade songs, and a real aquarium in which a goldfish seemed to be constantly gasping at the surface for breath while somebody played music off camera. His dad also bought the first air conditioners in town, for the living room and kitchen windows, and Vic liked the feeling of insulation they gave him. He didn't get much cold air in his bedroom unless he left the door open, but he liked hearing them groaning away in the house, and he could play the Magnavox and the Selmer louder without bugging the neighbors. Now that it was November, the windows were open again.

"Who'll replace my hubcaps?" his father asked over supper.

"They haven't been stolen yet," his mother said.

"But they will be," his dad said. "It's guaranteed."

"Use my car," Vic offered.

"You have to go in early. I got no use for standing around that school."

"I'll take the scooter," Vic offered.

"No, you're playing. It's your night, and you shouldn't have to show up with the horn tied on a scooter. Besides, it would be giving in to a gang of hoods, invisible hoods. I don't know how they do it, but they're not gonna get away with it this time."

"What'll you do?" Val asked, provocative as always, hoping to see some interesting trouble.

"I knew that dog would come in handy for something," his father said.

His mother made a hissing sound, like a librarian, but with more expression. "You're not taking that dog to the school," she said, and his father didn't answer.

Vic laughed, but he was nervous. He didn't care much for "Beautiful Colorado," but he'd worked on it pretty hard, and he was going to be standing out there solo. It was an easy audience, but it was an audience, and Branthooven had invited the band director from Florida State. Vic didn't know if the guy was coming all the way from Tallahassee just to hear him or had business here anyway, but FSU was one of the scholarships he'd been offered.

He excused himself from the table and brushed his teeth. He put on the heavy wool band uniform, the one they wore in all weather, including the nine or ten sweltering months of every year in Florida.

Maybe his dad's air-conditioning had spoiled him, but it seemed crazy to be wearing something in a tropical climate that could withstand a Russian winter. His chest glittered with contest ribbons, much like one of those dopey Russian heroes in the "Grin and Bear It" comic strip, with the caption that read "IS BIG IMPORTANT HERO OF PEOPLE." At least it was cool outside on that November night, and he drove to school with his windows open. Maybe they'd leave the auditorium doors open, too, and it would feel a little like Colorado.

The band room was the usual buzz and bustle. People didn't kid with him as usual because he had a solo tonight. Actually, most of the kids gave him lots of room anyway because of the trouble he'd taken to establish his coolness, and this was one time he regretted it. Vic realized how much he loved these smells and noises, the instruments and their players a precise and almost military hardware in the hands of children, some of whom, like Jimmy Johanssen— at that moment pretending his snare drum stand was a stick shift— might never grow up.

And he wished they wouldn't. He wished it would always be autumn in the most important year of their lives, with a concert or football game or even a parade ahead, so that the future could never come and would thus remain forever unspoiled. He smelled the wool of the other band members' uniforms in the cool breeze from the open band room door—like cedar closets, mothballs, sweaters, and the preserved cuddly toys of babies—and felt an embarrassing affection for all of them—not just Baz warming up on "Move" or Jimmy downshifting for a curve at Sebring or Cleaver goosing Margaret Droesch with his slide for the hundredth time, but Margaret, too, and Clarice Higbee, who had converted to the glockenspiel from accordion, and Dover Dunlap hitting his sousaphone bell on the top of the instrument room door for the *two* hundredth time, and Branthooven warning Dunlap for the one hundred and ninety-ninth time.

Branthooven's normally dark, camel-like face was shaven close tonight and maybe powdered, too. His eyes questioned Vic—are you ready?—and Vic nodded and put a little juice into his warm-up. For the first time Vic wondered what would make a man devote his life to this. Why worry about these goofy kids? Why shave twice and powder your face with Old Spice after-shave talc and give your-self the innocent look of a boy on his first prom date for this gang of doofi? Or was it doofuses? What made this work? What he felt now felt like love. For what? For Sousa and the small-time cats who wrote the concert band originals and arrangements of classical numbers they played? For Gershwin, maybe, Rodgers, Bernstein, but not for old John Philip. Maybe for playing itself? Surely not for one another?

Vic felt isolated, like a ghost or one of the dead people in *Our Town*. He wanted to touch them, but unnoticed. He wanted to say what they meant to him, but not be heard. He wanted to tell them this was all special, but he wouldn't have done it in a dozen lifetimes. He was afraid of embarrassing himself and was glad for Branthooven's rap of the baton, the usual mild scolding and pep talk, the caution about making a dignified passage to the auditorium—no screeching tire or duck noises. He was glad when Branthooven asked for concert B-flat to tune and they all gave it to him truly, because there were tears in Vic's eyes. It must be the weather, he thought.

Their passage to the auditorium was decent, if not militarily precise. Johanssen had one absolutely unbeatable noise—that of a puppy being stepped on—but while he knew it would crack everybody up, he also knew that Branthooven knew that only he could make it, and doing it meant he'd be not only without a car but without a car substitute, and God knew where his crazy hands would take him then. When the crowd in front of the building saw them filing in through the back door, they began putting out their cigarettes and making their entry through the front. Vic looked for his dad's 98 but couldn't spot it.

Inside, they tuned again, then began the "Stars and Stripes Forever" theme that they usually played to warm up the audience while folks settled in. The principal told the ushers to leave both front and rear doors open. Then Mr. Branthooven introduced Vic—the principal—the band—section leaders standing for a brief bow—and the first number, a medley from *West Side Story* that everybody liked. Johanssen got a chance to wail on congas, Baz got a muted solo on "Maria," and Vic had an eight-bar written solo on "Somewhere." He stretched it, doing some things of his own without making it sound too jazzy, and Branthooven let it go. As they put "Beautiful Colorado" on their stands, Vic saw his parents and sister come in late.

"Beautiful Colorado" was a waltz. After an introduction that involved the whole band, the others played background to his solo—and to what at first was only a spooky, unidentifiable banshee-like wail coming from God knew where, but itself more or less in three-four time. Vic found it was possible to retreat behind the almost automatic performance of this much-practiced piece and wonder what the strange noise was. It sounded familiar. And when he saw his father leave the auditorium—his mother's face hidden (but red, he knew) behind her program—he knew it was Senator McCarthy, probably chained to the rear axle and by then wrapped at least once around every tire and singing with just a few links of chain left between him and the asphalt, to the song he knew so well.

Vic almost laughed. He did, in fact, leak air through his nose and around his embouchure in a kind of explosive but contained laugh, but he kept on playing. And since the audience saw he was not embarrassed but was enjoying it himself, he had them where he wanted them. For one of the few times in his career, he played with the full, classical alto saxophone sound. McCarthy's yowls were cut short with a yelp like Johanssen's puppy just as Vic began to climb the ladder to the special-fingering A above high C. And though his father missed the actual moment, he was back in time to hear the applause, which drowned out Senator McCarthy's muted performance from inside the car.

In fact, the audience loved the coincidence of comedy and musicianship, and the applause continued until Mr. Branthooven, realizing that something beyond his standing for another mere bow would be required, gave in to showmanship himself and had Vic step forward to the microphone. "Thank you," Vic said. "The dog and I will be appearing next Saturday night—" And he let it go, riding back to his seat on the warm wave of laughter, thinking, this is a pretty good night for a square gig.

At the end of every concert they played the alma mater Miss Cook had written with an English teacher, now retired:

Boca Chica, alma mater, sternly tender ever be.
Teaching true and well life's lessons, shaping strong our
    destiny.
Boca Chica, alma mater, symbolized in gold and white.
May we always keep you stainless, ever aligned with truth
    and right.

After it was over, Vic walked with his family to the car, fighting
off an unreasonable fear that they would never do anything like this
again, that it was all changed now but they just hadn't been told.
Even his sister literally patted him on the back. When they got to
the Olds, Senator McCarthy had slobbered up the insides of all the
windows and chewed one of the first padded dashboards to come out
of Detroit. And all four hubcaps were gone, locks and all.

"I hope you make a lot of money playing that thing, kid," his
father said. "And soon."

                  That night Vic read in *Portrait of the Artist As a
Young Man:* "I will tell you what I will do and what I will not do. I will
not serve that in which I no longer believe, whether it call itself my
home, my fatherland, or my church: and I will try to express myself
in some mode of life or art as freely as I can and as wholly as I can,
using for my defense the only arms I allow myself to use—silence,
exile and cunning. . . .

"Amen. So be it. Welcome, O life! I go to encounter for the mil-
lionth time the reality of experience and to forge in the smithy of my
soul the uncreated conscience of my race.

"Old father, old artificer, stand me now and ever in good stead."

When the Saints

Go Marchin' In

On the night of the last home game of that season, the band was restless. Or at least Vic and his friends were. This had been far too ordinary an autumn for seniors who would never have another season like it. Or at least Vic thought so. Branthooven didn't even mind anymore when they sang "Turtle Wax," "This Is Very Poor" (to the tune of the Volga boatmen's song), or the Viking call to Odin ("Where the hell is Odin?"). These regular band japes were now traditions, just as was the confusion over whether the Boca Chica athletic teams were Saints or Vikings. The first Boca Chica students had chosen Vikings first, then learned of a team in Eau Gallie by that name and chose Saints, imposing one hagiology or history upon another. Both had taken, so they now did cheers and band numbers as Saints and as Vikings, and when the sportswriters complained, the principal, an Auburn graduate in physical education himself, pointed to the War Eagle/Tigers.

The Odin chant was from the Viking mythos, but the most fun

for Vic was the Dixieland version of "The Saints Go Marchin' In" that Vic, Baz, Johanssen, and Cleaver played, with Dumb-ass Dover Dunlap on sousaphone and Estrellita DeGomez playing on clarinet a memorized part Vic had written out for her. The kids ate it up and demanded it at least once every quarter of the game. And Baz played the "Fight" fanfares with the first-chair trumpet, a nerdling brownnoser band captain named Spencer Hathaway.

Sometimes they watched the game. Always Vic smelled the woolen uniforms, the cold air, the peanuts and cotton candy and candied apples sold by boosters of various clubs. The candied apples sometimes became dangerous missiles in the hands of junior high kids who came to the games only to cause trouble—looking up skirts from beneath the grandstands and bleachers, setting off fire-crackers, smoking cigarettes, trying to play their own games with footballs improvised of toilet paper rolls stolen from the men's rooms until the off-duty cops chased them out. If they were lucky, they saw panties or scored a direct hit with a candied apple missile. If they were unlucky, the cops got them. If they were really unlucky, they wandered near the Saint/Viking end zone, where Mickey Moran waited to kick anybody's ass that made his jaw feel tight.

Vic loved all this, and because he loved it (he couldn't explain why) he wanted something memorable to happen on this glorious, rare, autumn night—possibly the last like it many of them would see, unless they wanted to return like the ghostly grads who'd been launched from earlier classes into the world of the fuuuture and were now reading gas meters for the city or selling hosiery at Monkey Wards or pumping gas. What if this group was destined to end up that way? They needed something special to make them smile years from now, remembering the time they broke the system, the time the anarchy of their youth was still powerful enough to monkey-wrench a well-planned adult gig.

Like any good plan it was fairly simple (he had learned this from his conqueror reading) and virtually impossible to pin on anyone. It took only him, Baz, Johanssen, and Cleaver to agree that when they reached the sixteenth bar of the drum cadence that would bring them onto the field at halftime, they would each turn in a different direction. Vic would do a left flank march from his spot on the right.

Baz would turn right flank from the left. Cleaver, in the front row of trombones, took the biggest chance, because he would stop and march in place, allowing his advancing column to pile up behind him. And Johanssen would do a right oblique, suggesting that they'd already reached midfield and Spencer Hathaway, who was also the drum major, had given the signal to start their first formation: a hula hoop. If ever a formation deserved to be sabotaged, it was this one.

The first version had been for Cleaver to march to the rear, but it made him too conspicious, and he had some scholarships to protect, too. In the revised plan, he could claim he saw Hathaway signal. Branthooven marched to the left-front of the band and wouldn't see it anyway. Hathaway was the most likely goat for this, so he probably wouldn't be believed if he snitched. In the yearbook he listed his future plans "in Life" as "music and politics."

It was subtle and beautiful, and catastrophic. The kids in the grandstand, who seldom looked at the band, now looked at the band—held peanuts halfway to mouths or cotton candies at a safe distance from sweaters until they could see just what was going on out there, where even the drum cadence seemed to have collapsed. Even the toilet paper football–playing junior high kids stopped to gawk, and that allowed Mick Moran, Junior Hazlewood, and the other rats to capture a few of them for torture and later release. As Vic changed directions several times after the initial signal, he thought, Mad Moped Max would have a name for this. Something in physics. Not about things getting colder, damn him, but about things getting crazy, heating up, bouncing off one another, making people notice.

The casualties were higher than expected. Betty Lou Burak, Frank Finney, and Lisa Glatt all got fat lips, having misinterpreted the chaos as a signal to begin playing the "Hula Hoop Song." Meredith Moraine and Laura Raspberry got hooked or poked in the face by wildly swinging necks and mouthpieces—tenor sax and clarinet, respectively. And the tall and gawky former accordionist *cum* glockenspielist, Clarice Higbee, was hit by Dover Dunlap's out-of-control sousaphone bell and knocked colder than a tombstone.

The best thing they could think of to do—Vic was by then helping, very sorry he'd done the thing—was to move awkwardly into their hula hoop formation and, once the stretcher bearers had borne away the unconscious Clarice, to wherever injured glockenspielists are taken, resume their practiced routine. Hathaway was angry but could prove nothing. Branthooven seemed beyond anger. He seemed ashamed, depressed. Vic was ashamed, too. The band seemed to have lost its spirit, something the irresponsible pranksters hadn't even thought it had, or would miss. The planners of the coup never mentioned it to one another again, and the Saints/Vikings lost the game, 21–6.

Baz had a six-pack in a cooler in the trunk of his Plymouth. Vic had left the Olds at home, concerned about his own hubcaps now. They went to the A in their band uniforms, but it was a listless evening and people seemed to shun them. Baz went to the men's room out back and didn't return. Vic wondered how long he would have to keep taking care of these people. Behind the A he saw a circle of rats drawn up around little Baz, who had the also diminutive Junior Hazlewood in a headlock and was singing the filthy lyrics to "Bernie's Tune" as Junior turned in a growing panic with this new and more dangerous kind of freak attached to him.

Moran's jaw was loose. "Junior told your friend the band sucked," Mick said, laughing, his tongue showing pink in the neon.

"The band does suck," Vic said, then changed his mind. "The band doesn't suck." He said it straight to Mick, who laughed and showed more of his tongue.

Baz seemed to be enjoying his ride by now, experiencing for the first time in his life the thrill of even a fleeting physical superiority over another of God's flawed creatures. "Any requests?" Baz asked Junior. "I know a lot of tunes."

"Shut up," Junior mumbled, muffled in Saint/Viking wool, learning the price for challenging a newly awakened school spirit. "Make him shut up!"

"Say 'uncle,'" Baz said, perhaps going too far, and certainly too far back in the slang repertoire.

"*Jesus*," Junior yelled through the wool coat. "He's crazy!"

"Give up?" Baz asked, his trampled white bucks now resting on the shell lot as Junior's exhaustion and panic began to tell.

"That's enough," Mick said.

Baz surprised him. "He has to say quit."

Mick thought that was hilarious. "You quit, Junior?" he asked, laughing, and Junior took the offer, no doubt planning to plead insanity on the part of his opponent.

"I quit. Now get this crazy fucker off me."

They drank another six-pack before Baz dropped him off at home. They still had not mentioned the stampede, but Vic felt they'd stood up for the band in their own way, and everybody would forget about it soon. He called Clarice Higbee's house and asked if she was OK, and her sleepy mother said she was.

In bed, the beer and adrenaline were still working on him. He read *On the Road:* "The only people for me are the mad ones, the ones who are mad to live, mad to talk, mad to be saved, desirous of everything at the same time, the ones who never yawn or say a commonplace thing, but burn, burn, burn like fabulous yellow roman candles exploding like spiders across the stars and in the middle you see the blue centerlight pop and everybody goes 'Awww!'"

And then, in *The March of the Barbarians:* "The Egyptian army had, in fact, grown out of slaves—the warriors known as *mamluks* (the possessed ones—the "Mamelukes"). In the beginning, the mamluks had been boys bought as slaves and trained in arms, to serve the shadow kalifs of Kahirah (Cairo) as a bodyguard—young Bulgars, Turks, Circassians and Georgians purchased in the slave markets of the nearer east. They were, therefore, scions of the white race—for the Turks were white—who knew no other profession than that of war. The most daring of them were known as the White Slaves of the River.

"And, like those other Turks who had first served and then dominated the kalifs of Baghdad, the mamluks had soon made figureheads of the weaker kalifs of Kahirah. Their *corps d'elite* became the *halka*, or Guard.

"From the first inroads of the Mongols, the ranks of the mamluks had been enlarged by Turkish elements uprooted in Kwaresmia and the Black Sea region, particularly by those wayward souls the

73

Turkomans of the White and the Black Sheep. One member of this turbulent fellowship had the hardihood to believe the Mongols could be defeated. . . .

"He is Baibars—the Panther—better known by his nickname of the Crossbowman. And Friar William of Tripoli, who knew much of him, relates that as a soldier he was not inferior to Julius Caesar, nor did he yield in malignity to Nero.

"In person he is a Kipchak Turk, more than six feet tall, with one eye whitened by the scar that blinded it. He wields his sword with his left hand, and he delights in covering his body with gorgeous silks. His dossier informs us that as a boy Baibars was conscripted by a Mongol army—taken captive, and sold by Venetian slave merchants in the market of Damascus for about ninety dollars, rejected by the purchaser by reason of his blind eye, taken as a slave by a mamluk amir. But Baibars knows the Mongol army and its methods, from bitter experience. . . .

"With a following of Turks he defeats the host of the allied Crusaders at Gaza. By expedient of a counter-attack—a lesson learned from the Mongols—he has managed to break the heart of Louis, king of the French, and to repel a French crusade at Mansura. With Kutuz and a girl named Pearl Spray, he holds at his wayward disposition the nearer east—until the coming of his former masters, the Mongols."

The beer didn't help, nor did the reading. When he fell asleep much later he could still see Branthooven's long, grieving camel's face, and all night he dreamed of armies marching in all directions at once, dressed in golden wool, devastating their own ranks with misdirected instruments, marching in their bloody white bucks over their own casualties as they turned the well-marked gridiron into a muddy swamp, a killing field.

Straight, No Chaser

The baritone surprised Buster and the other cats. Baz was at the Cypress Room, too, that Saturday night, either on or off duty at the morgue—maybe not even he knew. Mad Max, in his usual spot, viewed the big new horn with his usual sardonic detachment. Vic was having fun, drinking what he felt like drinking, even joking with the crowd. Somehow the physically heavy horn was psychologically lighter, and he felt like an athlete who trained with weights, after the weights were removed.

Everything was the same except the size of the horn and the fact that it was an octave lower. Same key, same fingering, but not the same celebrity expectations that the alto brought with it. They played "Straight, No Chaser," and for the first time ever Vic felt like a part of Buster's band. He got a solo and even did some playful bebop honking in the lower registers, goosing the crowd. At the break he ordered, for the first time in his life, a shot of bourbon. He drank it off, smiling at Max, then coughed and swallowed some of the ginger ale Max offered. Tonto played a little riff like a siren in a British cop movie and Vic looked over to the bandstand. Tonto waved him over.

He thought Tonto would be happier than anybody about the change, but he wasn't. "You skatin', man, bringin' that big piece of plumbin' in here. It's time for our little talk."

"Doesn't it sound OK?" Vic asked.

"I guess it does if you a plumber," Tonto said.

"I can play solos better," Vic said. "Ad-libbing comes easier. Maybe it's my natural horn."

"And maybe plumbin's your natural trade," Tonto said, and Vic could see he was really upset. "I just about got you ready to listen, then you go hidin' on me with that thing."

"I'll listen."

Tonto took a big breath, then put his horn down across his open case. "Dig," he said, then picked it up again. "This is your horn. You don't walk away. You do it right. Now I'm gonna hip you what 'right' is. First, you learn every damn thing that horn can do, forwards, backwards, *every* which way. That's what Bird did, Cannonball, that Quill cat you talk about. You learn to read and you learn all the chords, every goddamn one of them, by heart, so it's in your fingers. You learn all the chords in every key. Then you learn every song you might ever play, and you learn to play it in every key you might have to play it in. You practice every day. The method books'll get you around most of the things you gonna run into, but here we do some cute stuff, so you learn that too. You already done most of this, but you don't dig how important it is."

"Why do I choke on alto?" Vic asked. "Why do I run out of ideas and play shit, just faking until somebody else takes over? Why do I dry up?"

" 'Cause you human," Tonto said angrily. "God*damn* it, I dry up, too, I fake, I fall back. I scuffle."

"I never heard you do it."

"That's 'cause I don't make it obvious. I only been playin' about twelve years, and Bird only played about twenty 'fore he died. So shit, how come you can't come along and just cut us after your short time? I do wonder 'bout that. Where you think talent comes from, boy?"

"From birth, I guess." Vic was getting the secret, and it scared him.

"That's *raw* talent. And there's also such a thing as genius. Cat like Bird went farther than most 'cause he had special gifts, but he had to learn the horn so it worked as easy as his mouth, easier. Stitt learn it that way, Desmond, Adderley, Pepper. I learn it that way. I ain't no slouch. Maybe they never gonna call me a genius, but if they don't it ain't gonna be 'cause I *quit!* You see, you don't know! You ain't the one to judge. Your obligation is to do it as well as you can, and that's *all* it is."

"I gotta judge myself," Vic said, his neck warm.

"No, you *don't!* Not that way. You sittin' on your own shoulder, judging every damn note before it even come out. That's a tight-ass, white, ofay way of playin'. Nobody good can play that way. Nor they can't fight that way nor thow a football nor even make love that way. You work your chops up as best you can, then you get the *hell* out the way and let 'em play."

"But what *about* when I just dry up?" Vic thought he had Tonto there.

"Like I said, you fall back. Everybody got a few riffs they can fall back on, rest with, and just wait for the next good idea. You gotta believe it's comin', and *that*, my friend, is a big part of it."

"Bird doesn't fall back. Quill doesn't."

"You listen," Tonto said, grinning. "I got you now. You listen and I know you'll hear it. We all got our little deals we can hide behind, little automatic stuff like we do in talkin'. The pros just learn to make it look like part of the whole, straight-ahead brilliant plan. That's why they're pros."

Vic nodded, looking into Tonto's eyes. He thought he heard one of Bird's backup riffs in his mind. Then he recognized one of Quill's. Maybe. Then somebody played Mose Allison again on the box and "Seventh Son" stole the music from his head.

"You see, I gotcha, don't I?" Tonto said, grinning. "And looka-here, you don't always got to be playin' straight ahead. Leave some space, let some time go by if you ain't sure. Like Buster says, if you in doubt, stay out. Listen to the great old tenor men for that. Hawkins, Lester. They don't have to be honkin' every second.

Silence is music, too. You ain't got to worry. Your talent will think of somethin'. And once you got the technique cold, try singin' your ideas with records. Nice and relaxed. Then see can you play 'em on the horn. If you can't sing it, you can't play it. That's a way to try out your ideas without gettin' hung up in the horn. Dig?"

"It's scary, thinking you have to trust it like that all the time."

Tonto let a few of his own beats go by. "That's why we juice," he said. "That's why some of us use dope. You notice I say some of *us*. That's a compliment, or maybe I should send you a telegram. Sure it's scary, but we get to fly. I think we can fly without dope, without juice. I don't use it much."

"You have to trust talent? But I hear Bird do things I can't imagine ever doing. Quill, too. I mean I can't hear myself ever getting there."

"I'm going to give you directions right now to *there*," Tonto said. "Same as to Carnegie Hall. How do I get to Carnegie Hall, class?"

"Practice," Vic said, coming in with the old punch line.

Tonto nodded and grinned. "That's right. Practice and faith. And a little mercy and luck don't hurt, either. That's how it come to all of us, even Bird. You just play and practice *all* the time, and if you lucky one day you find you not only got a voice of your own, but you got something to say. And I don't mean cuteness, fancy licks. I don't even necessarily mean the blues, 'cause they only the start. They not the message but the *cause* of the message. The only real soul, the only idea worth sayin', is love. If you lucky, one day you hear it come out your horn.

"I gotta whiz while the colored sign's on the door, so to speak. Nice talkin' to you."

Vic went back to the bar and had another shot, this time with a beer chaser. Mad Moped Max took the stool next to him and began to talk, as if to himself or nobody in particular. Vic heard some of it, but mainly he was thinking about what Tonto said. He wished people would leave the goddamn jukebox alone and stop talking to him so he could think things through. This was important, the key to the whole riddle. His head was hot.

"The second law of thermodynamics," Max was saying. "The universe is a closed system. So entropy takes over, everything gets slowly colder, until we freeze over. 'Course it'll take millions of years, so it's no reason to go home early . . . Mankind's acting like a slime mold. We're eatin' up our planet without a thought to where future meals are comin' from. When the slime mold colony starts to run out of food, it puts up a column and spits spores out, so some of them can maybe find new food sources and start new colonies. That's the unconscious motive behind our goddamned space program . . . Now the next interesting spot's Cuba. Castro hasn't got a chance there. He won't even have time to change his magazine subscriptions over to the palace before *his* ass is grass. Only question is will it be our newest state, which makes a certain kind of sense, or another tinhorn dictator to keep watch on the guinea gangsters' business. The Illuminati decide those things. I'm just your ordinary genius with no power of my own . . . We'll have men walking on the moon within ten years, and I helped put 'em there. Sounds impossible, but impossible's no longer the problem. Almost everything's becoming possible except wisdom. Old-fashioned wisdom, which is exactly what we do need to keep from possibilitying ourselves into a piece of burned-out space garbage. Once the rockets go up, who cares where they come down? That's not my department says Wernher von Braun. No, wisdom's the thing, the serenity to accept the things we cannot change, the courage to change the things we can, and the wisdom to know the difference. That's why I quit. You can't program wisdom, especially if you don't have it. Garbage in, garbage out . . . 'Course modern life's a lot like tryin' to stuff spaghetti up a cat's ass anyway, but who am I to complain? . . . We're gonna have computers we can carry in briefcases. Shockley showed us how, but the military's glommed onto it first. We'll be able to—"

Vic split for the next set and missed what they'd be able to do. Was Max drinking again? Was the guy nuts or queer or what?

He blew a great set and had two more shots before going out to the beach with the band. Baz, already there, passed a J to him. He took a good hit, passed it to Baltimore, looked out at the quiet Gulf and up at the silent stars. "Yeah, Bird," Hush was saying.

Before he realized what he was doing, Vic said, "Quill cuts Bird." Suddenly it had seemed important to assert that, but it was also, in this company, even without Ice, nearly suicidal. "Say what?" Buster asked, then chuckled.

Vic went right ahead, like a cliff diver sailing out over the rocks.

"They actually met, I heard, in Atlantic City. Place owned by some boxer. And Gene blew Bird right off the stand."

"Aww, man," Tonto said, leaving the circle to raise his hands to the sky, asking God to witness this sad white boy spectacle.

"Easy, man," Baz said.

"Where you hear that?" Buster asked.

The waves rolling in said "Hush."

"I don't know," Vic said. "I just heard it. And I believe it. Nobody's saying Bird isn't great, but somebody's got to be better some day. I say it happened."

"Don't give him any more of this shit," Buster said, not unfriendly. "Some people hallucinate on this tea. See, man," he continued. "Quill just a feather, dig. With Parker you got the whole bird."

"Hush," said the waves again.

"Bird's great," Vic said, an unregenerate apostate, "but Quill cuts him. Even Bird's widow, Chan, said Quill had more soul than Woods, the cat she married next."

"But that's Woods, a white cat," Buster said. "Not Bird. Where you gettin' this trash?"

"So that's what it comes to," Vic said. "White, black. Quill played on some of Billie Holiday's recordings. Just lately. Maybe she don't know soul, either."

"Which ones?" Ernie asked, something of a scholar.

"I think I heard him on 'Sometimes I'm Happy' and 'You Took Advantage of Me,'" Vic said. Suddenly his head and body felt all hollow, and his voice echoed through him, frightening him for the first time that night.

"Aw, man, you dreamin'," Hush said. "Let's go in and play. And forget all this happened."

Vic recovered from the hollowness. He felt hard, almost mean, in his rebellion, and he played an angry set for Quill, not backing down, driven by his wild assertions to try to live up to them. Sometime during that set, Tonto said to him: "You wailin'. Maybe there some soul in there after all."

Sometime later in that set Vic stopped being conscious of what he was doing and remembered nothing else until he felt someone dragging him from beneath a car. Then nothing, until he came to in

Max's apartment. He drank coffee. Max told him he'd gone to sleep in the parking lot and somebody had parked over him. "I'm gonna take you home, but you have to be able to get in. I don't want to explain this to your parents."

Then there was some weird business of maps—Max showing him Italy with two overlays, one where the hard-drinking un-self-reflective Roman Legions mustered out and the other where the highest incidence of alcoholism was. The two hardly touched. "See," Max was saying, "sensitive, artistic, intelligent people don't survive in the legion. Where the legions mustered out you don't see much alcoholism. Where the sensitive, talented people are it's all red. Do you see what I'm telling you? There are different kinds of survival, different kinds of fitness. We wouldn't be good soldiers, but that doesn't mean we have to be drunks. I can do the same map thing with the samurai in Japan."

Vic wouldn't have been surprised to see Max do anything at that point. He wasn't even sure this wasn't all a dream. He vaguely remembered Max driving his Olds home and talking to a cop, Crump, who'd stopped it thinking he'd bust Vic again only to find this strange new puzzle, the old crewcut guy who showed him this serious-looking federal ID and promised to take responsibility for the boy's safety. Later, Crump thought he should have run them both in, except that the guy was probably some homo working the beach bars, in which case the punk was getting what he deserved.

Vic didn't know how Max got home. Probably he had the moped in the trunk, and probably one of the neighbors had reported this burr-headed guy his dad's age pedaling away on it. Maybe Crump called his dad.

His father sat down at the breakfast table the next morning after noon, after Vic had been sick again, this time with grape juice. "You'll have to leave," his dad said. "I'll give you a week to find a place. You can keep the car and scooter, but you have to make your own money. Your mom wants you to come home for Christmas dinner."

It seemed a continuation of the nightmarish visions of last night, but gradually he realized it was, like much of what he remembered, real. He thought briefly about calling Max, but he didn't want any more maps or weird theories. He called Baz instead, and Baz called his boss, and the boss offered Vic the other cot over the prep room in exchange for the same duties Baz performed. There was a small salary, what Baz called "short bread," and, he joked, very few tips. Vic hoped Buster could afford to pay him a little now. He packed the car with his records, books, and clothes, saying he'd come back for the scooter if he needed it, and drove away. His mother and sister were crying, and his dad was in the garage.

That night in the morgue dormitory he drank six beers, enjoying a little this new freedom, and smoked a joint with Baz. In his sax case he found another note: "Mom's been putting ipecac in the juice, hoping it would cure you. Please don't go bad. We love you. Val." Later, on his cot, he read *The Earth Is the Lord's:* "Kurelen had told Temujin: 'The day a man doth realize that he hath no friends is the day he is delivered from his swaddling clothes.' . . .

"He was suddenly aware of some terrible Presence, of some unsleeping Eye, some most ominous regard. For an instant, his heart quailed, and his hand dropped. Then, lifting his eyes, he gazed at the brightening immensity of the skies, and his whole spirit was filled with triumph and defiance, fury and savage joy.

" 'I have the world!' he cried, and his voice seemed to sound like a trumpet note in the silence. 'I, Genghis Khan, am the world!'

"Only silence answered him, unbroken and contemptuous and awesome. Only the silence of God replied. The sun rose above the broken horizon. It fell with a bloody light upon the face and the figure of Genghis Khan. And suddenly, about him, there seemed a spectral horde, the shadows of the past and the shadows of the future, the shadows of the enemies of men.

"They stood about him, silent and fierce, seeing, but unseen.

"And the eyes of God saw everything, and the silence of God swallowed up the universe, and the spirit of God seemed to flow out upon the earth, invincible and conquering, and ever victorious."

The Christmas Song

Baz warned him it was the suicide season, but neither of them had been through it before, and neither of them expected the sheer business of death that time of year—especially in Florida, which is for many, sadly, the last chance for happiness. About 70 percent of them were already dead and went straight to the prep room for Doug Armstrong, red-haired, freckle-faced, all-American mortician. The others they took to the emergency room at Mound Park or St. Anthony's, the one who wasn't driving administering such first aid as he could. Doug had put Baz through a short course, and Baz had instructed Vic, which was to say that Vic knew next to nothing. He read up in the manual while Baz practiced muted, but nothing could have prepared him for what came.

The most common cause, or tool, was booze and pills, and one of the most common side effects was projectile vomiting—the body's own stomach pump. Vic's first run was to a beach cottage where the wife of a psychiatrist lay in a bed from which she had vomited on the ceiling, probably saving her own life but making a mess. Suicide was seldom neat. Those who tried to spare others the unpleasantness waded into the Gulf and were washed up days later with crabs attached, or wandered into the pine woods and pulled a trigger, only to be found by kids following the smell and body-bagged in pieces.

But it wasn't all suicide. They had one murder, or attempted murder. A separated man and wife met at Wolfie's deli in the holiday spirit to discuss reconciliation. The talks didn't go well, and the woman took a .22 revolver from her purse and shot the man in the center of his forehead. Vic found the woman in the parking lot, dazed. They'd arrived before the police, so he took the pistol from her limp grip. Inside, Baz found the man alive. The bullet had not been strong enough to penetrate his skull and had traveled a furrow around to exit just before the artery in his temple. As Baz tried to bandage him, he requested aspirin. "I'm getting a bitch of a headache," he said.

And Vic delivered a baby, or did most of it—leaving the cord to the emergency room personnel—and did it, to his great surprise, from what he'd learned in an Erpi Classroom Film. "When that Aprill," he thought.

What of the 70 percenters—those beyond help—or those who died in the Christmas season of natural causes? They must be cared for, too. One did his best for the dead and the families of the dead, even when he wanted instead to cry, to go home to tell his parents. Even for the poor man whose circulatory system was so sclerotic that the somewhat tinted (for a healthy complexion) embalming fluid went too much to some parts and too little to others, so that he turned all bright red and green and had to be redone by Doug in sections, and was named Mr. Christmas. One learned to laugh. One learned to say "one" instead of more personal pronouns, because this shocking, sad Christmas had become almost more personal than he could stand, and one needed distance.

Or maybe he needed to be close. On one of his few days off he called Emily. To his surprise, she agreed to come to the dormitory above the prep room. Baz took the ambulance to visit a woman he was seeing who called funeral homes and late-night DJs and invited them over. She had a police scanner, so he wouldn't miss any calls.

Emily asked for a tour. Then she drank some of the grape juice and grain alcohol punch he'd mixed up in the embalming pump—just a few sips, for the novelty, like a fraternity gross-out—and they made love like more or less normal, living people on his cot, though he did wear protection. He had Mel Tormé on the Magnavox, singing "The Christmas Song." "Chestnuts roasting on an open fire. Jack Frost nipping at your nose."

Emily had her own car by then, a tiny Nash Metropolitan her daddy bought her after she'd broken up with Billy for the second time. Presumably it was Billy who'd taught her to make love more or less like normal people as they just had, for the first time in Vic's life. Vic thought she was pretty casual about the whole thing. She said to call her, but she didn't seem anxious about it. Vic thought, maybe she's the teacher.

"I'm growing up too fast," he told Baz after one especially messy call.

"I'm hip," said Baz, "but it ain't nothin' but the blues."

"The blues is enough," Vic said.

He had Christmas dinner at home. His mother said to invite his friend, Basil. It was a little awkward. They asked him what his job was like and whom he'd seen, and he could only say, the usual. They had candied yams with pecans and oyster stuffing—two of his favorite things. Baz was very polite, though he ate like a Viking. He thanked Vic's mother for the "sumptuous repast." Vic's dad rolled his eyes and Val giggled. His mother gave him a sweater. His sister, who had made the cheerleading squad for next year and quit band, gave him her Selmer clarinet. His father said it looked like the end of Mrs. Messenger's Trained Performing Human Children as a team and gave him a Duke Ellington LP. And Baz got the all-purpose bottle of Old Spice, which he claimed never to have smelled before, and perhaps hadn't.

This Time the

Dream's on Me

On another rare day off before New Year's Eve, Vic stopped in at the Blue Room on U.S. 19 to see Chick Czement, the blind, white organist from Detroit. Chick had a strange sense of humor—half hip, half corn—but he was one of the best of that odd breed, the lounge keyboard artist, and the Blue Room crowd loved him. He lived in a room in the back and had been there for three years. Vic had his Selmer in the Olds, bringing it back from a pad job at Lefter's Music, and he thought that if Chick was warming up for happy hour they could play a little.

He heard the organ and, as his eyes adjusted from the afternoon sun to the lounge light, a tasty woman's voice. It sounded like June Christy. It was Betty Boop, singing "You're My Thrill." Vic joined the scattered applause from the help and a few drinkers. Boop smiled at him. She wasn't wearing her auburn wig or lipstick, and there was no Ice today. "Hello," Vic said. "Chick Czement, at his organ again." Another old joke, and delivered tentatively with Boop there.

"Don't tell me," Chick said. "It's my young friend RCA Victor, the saxophone prodigy. I'd like you to meet June Christy." Boop laughed. "I'm color-blind, you see. Listen, Victor, join us for a tune or two . . ." His right hand picked out the melody to "or three, or four, or more," and Boop joined him with "in Dreamland, with me and my gal." Chick moved into an intro for another song, pausing to give Vic a tuning note—uncanny hearing, or maybe he smelled the new oil and cork grease of the open case—and on into "This Time the Dream's on Me," another Christy favorite.

Vic went back to the storeroom door and warmed up into it until he felt a little like joining in, though Boop was intimidating. He tried to remember what Tonto had told him. He came up behind Chick's riser and Chick knew he was there and gave him a chorus. It wasn't too bad. The horn had been worked over nicely, every pad a precise fit, every moving part with its thin coating of fine oil. He played a little behind Boop's out chorus and thought it fitted in well enough. He'd always liked the key change Christy did near the end. "To see you through, 'till you're everything you want to be. It must be true, 'cause this time the dream's on me—ba da ba daa you be—this time the dream's on, baba daba dop, on me."

It felt good. Boop reached down and gave him a hand up to the riser. It wasn't necessary, but that felt even better. Chick was already moving into "But Not for Me," enjoying this unusual afternoon jam, and Boop made room beside her at the mike, encouraging him to do maybe more than background, but who knew because away they went and he forgot about it all when Boop nodded to give him a chorus and he felt her hand in the small of his back.

Magic. Pure magic. How could anything so simple make such a difference? Could heroin do this? He doubted it. He heard himself playing for the first time at a strange distance he'd gained with Boop's touch, as if he were listening now, as surprised as anyone— and it was surprising—at what was coming out. It felt like the descriptions he'd read of how space would feel to folks who'd fought gravity all their lives. One little push and you're gone, flying! There was joy in the horn, and not a drop of flop sweat, and he heard Chick give a little cry of delight and goose the organ just a little in a way that felt almost as good as Boop's hand, which somehow told him also her pleasure in the music he was making.

He played sixty-four bars of the first joy he'd had this grim season, but when Chick said "Go," Vic said "No more," afraid to jinx a perfect thing, but continued on equal and still joyful terms with Boop on her last chorus and, giddy with it, did one of those all-over-the-horn wind-down endings that finally faded into silence, and, not long after, loud voices yelling over hands clapping and a pot banging in the storage room and Boop's hand rubbing his back now and her voice laughing, and Chick saying, "Brothers and sisters, shall we pray? I wish we had a tape of this," and Boop laughing louder and her own voice saying, "I believe this young white honker boy alto got a Christmas *gift*," and Vic thinking: I can die right now and it's all OK.

The happy hour crowd was coming in, and they weren't color-blind like Chick, so Vic packed the horn and thanked him, and, without a word from either of them, he and Boop walked outside together. It was getting prematurely dark. "Go with me," he said.

"We got to be very careful," she said, but got into the Olds. "This is some crazy short. We couldn't flash more if we had some coon tails on the antenna. What kinda wheels are these, anyhow?"

"Conspicuous," he said, and she laughed. Then she frowned.

"Right. Now we can't go north 'cause there's no reason for coloreds to be there in a white car. Can't go west to the beach. Can't go downtown. Can't go south 'cause Ice might see or hear."

"We'll go south," he said.

"There won't be no explainin'. I've got to duck down when we go through the neighborhood. Maybe once we on the way to the bridge, out where it's mostly woods."

"Don't you put your head down," he said.

"Anybody asks you," she said. "I'm the cleanin' girl you takin' home."

"No you're not," he said.

She kept her head up, but he could tell she was scared. He had a pint of bourbon under the seat, and when they were clear he gave it to her and hit passing gear, and they rumbled along the new leg of what would be an interstate someday toward the bay and the new Skyway bridge. He slowed and turned right before that and drove through a network of perfect, pink cement roads built for a development that hadn't come in the 1920s but surely would now, and on to the gangster's house, right on the bay with a view of Egmont channel, pink tile roof and stucco exterior, abandoned, vandalized, filled with the ghosts of many other illicit deeds. Sunset.

He'd no sooner come to a stop than Boop hiked her skirt and pulled off her panties and he pulled down his jeans and jockey shorts and moved to her side, under her. And then he had her lips, whiskey-sweet, as she slid down onto him and her voice in his ear saying "Sweet boy, sweet, sweet boy," and both of them moved suddenly together crying out, and then, both finished quickly, her voice humming "Dream" and his lips on her neck kissing the tight, tiny curls and her skin, dark and warm as if holding the sun or generating its own mysterious velvet heat, and he thought: God, I have—Africa on my lap! I am with a *black* woman. I am *in* a black woman. Never in my wildest. Jesus.

She was really worried as he drove her home. She insisted he stop at 22nd Avenue and 34th Street and let her catch a black cab home. "Remember," she said. "I clean for you."

"My parents can't afford you."

"You can't afford me neither, honey, but that's another story."

He'd thought so. "I don't live at home. I live at a funeral home."

She didn't like that at all. "I don't work *there*," she said. "Just let me off."

He pulled behind the liquor store, hating for it to end this way. "This has got to be the only time for us," she said. She was getting herself together for the places he couldn't go. "But you are mighty sweet. I can't kiss you here but I want to touch you one more time. Just remember the sweet parts. Make it last. And this time I thank you for the nice ride."

She touched him. He didn't think it would be enough. He knew it wouldn't last. Then she got out of the Olds and walked around the corner to where she'd catch a cab, or maybe board the Frenchtown bus with the cleaning women waiting there.

Old Folks

Vic worked New Year's Eve, the worst grief so
far, and got the next day off. Aunt Glad and Uncle Homer had asked
him to New Year's dinner at Morrison's cafeteria. He hadn't seen
them in a long time, and Aunt Glad had bought him his sax, and he
loved their cracker kin-warmth despite their cracker meanness, so
he went.

"Hoppin' John," Uncle Homer said. "Can't be New Year's without
hoppin' John." Hoppin' John was black-eyed peas with ham hocks
on rice, covered with chopped raw onion and, in Uncle Homer's
case, Tabasco. Later, on the sidewalk outside Morrison's, Uncle
Homer would smoke a Picayune cigarette from Louisiana, because
Aunt Glad wouldn't let him smoke it anywhere else. Uncle Homer
was no ordinary redneck. He owned liquor stores all over town, and
the rumor was that in the 1930s, when he was just getting started,
he'd sold some bolita, and that when the Trafficantes sent a wise
guy over to muscle in on Uncle Homer's lottery business, Uncle

Homer blew him all the way out into the street with both barrels of twelve-gauge buckshot. Vic had never quite been able to believe that one, but Uncle Homer was an institution, like hoppin' John on New Year's, like Morrison's itself.

They went through the cafeteria line, Vic's taste buds remembering the batter-fried shrimp, okra fried or stewed with tomatoes, the pecan pie. He ordered the makings of hoppin' John himself. "I hope that nigger bitch from last time is gone," Aunt Glad said in a tone not too carefully lowered.

"Jefferson's here," Uncle Homer said. Jefferson would take care of everything. He'd been carrying trays here since Vic was old enough to remember. As long as Jefferson was there, Uncle Homer and Aunt Glad could enjoy Morrison's as the last vestige of a plantation culture they'd never known—nor their forebears, either, poor sharecroppers that they were. Jefferson remembered every little detail of their lives, knew the exact ages of their children and other young relatives, and boasted in his obsequious way of their accomplishments. Jefferson always made Vic feel like Gainesborough's "Blue Boy"—which hung in his parents' bedroom—or Little Lord Fauntleroy, or some Anglo-Saxon prince of that time now gone with the wind. Once or twice a week—or more often if they wanted or needed—Aunt Glad and Uncle Homer could drive downtown in the Cadillac to Morrison's and have this man named after (and maybe descended from) America's greatest polymath and Renaissance man as their servant. As Aunt Glad would and did often say, Jefferson was a good nigger who knew his place.

As they passed the sweetened and unsweetened iced tea, the cut lemon and lime wedges, and neared the cash register with trays overburdened, Jefferson was waiting. A wide grin showed gold fillings. He looked like Uncle Ben on the rice box. "Miz Glad, Mista Homa," he said, and it seemed he had never been happier to see anyone. Behind him, waiting to take the master and mistress's young nephew's tray, picking up a few spare bucks on a holiday, stood Tonto.

"And here's the young horn player, all growed up," Jefferson said. "A mighty fine lookin' young man." Tonto's face was unreadable as he carried Vic's tray. A corn stick fell over the side and Vic caught it, restoring it to its dish under Aunt Glad's stern gaze. It was painful to see Tonto here, painful not to acknowledge the man who'd probably taught him more about music *and* survival than anyone else, especially painful to see him nod in thanks, eyes lowered, like Bird on that Earl Wilson TV show, to Uncle Homer's generous tip. "That's a new boy," Aunt Glad said later. "You tipped him too much. I don't like his attitude."

There was no point in defending Tonto. Vic wouldn't do it. He would do what he figured Tonto did and make himself numb to this. He would answer Aunt Glad's questions politely and repeat his ritual amazement at Uncle Homer's copious use of Tabasco and try not to think, much less say, that he loved them with all his heart and hated them also, and that the man they were judging was worth a dozen crackers, or, for that matter, a dozen of the mythical southern aristocrats they needed to believe in to get through their own lives. It would never reach them. They hadn't even mentioned the fact that he'd been thrown out of his parents' house and was living above the prep room in a funeral home. They were the generation whose eyes would close forever before they saw Tonto or Jefferson or maybe even him, except *in extremis*, as fellow suffering souls. They had their ways.

And how easy it was for him. He'd enjoyed all the benefits of his secret discovery at a cost less than Uncle Homer's tip.

"What's that new boy's name?" Uncle Homer asked when Jefferson brought their coffee.

"Perkins," Jefferson said, and Vic realized it was the first time he'd heard Tonto's name. "He might work out," Jefferson continued, looking stern, "and then again he might not. You let me know, Mista Homa, if he don't please you."

Smoke Gets in Your Eyes

Home Room

Nothing but announcements and a sense of ac-
celeration, deadlines coming or already here or past, all moving
too fast.

Art

Down Beat

Doc Severinson directs NBC Orchestra for ailing
Skitch Henderson   east coast and west coast sidemen should
swap   the alto sax never seems in tune to me. It always
sounds sharp   *A Dictionary for Practical Cats* by Don
Freeman It is the custom nowadays in all books of jazz, and with
just about all the slick magazine pieces, to include a glossary of
jazz terms. This enables the lay reader to understand the

jazzman's quaint phraseology, which otherwise might be too—
that is to say, too far out. It narrows the gap between the jazzman
and his public, which is rather wide at times. . . . However,
there remains a conspicuous lack, and that is a glossary for the
jazzman. . . . HIP, n. Lateral part of the body between the brim
of the pelvis and the free part of the thigh. The hip joint is
between the hip bone and the femur. CAT, n. A domestic
carnivorous animal of the feline family   ALTO SAX 1. Paul
Desmond 1446   2. Lee Konitz 711   3. Art Pepper 639
4. Julian Adderley 472   5. Sonny Stitt 447   6. Johnny Hodges
405   7. Bud Shank 186   8. Phil Woods 120   9. Jackie
McLean 114   10. Benny Carter 99   11. Lennie Niehaus 84
12. John La Porta 78   13. Gene Quill 75

Johnny Richards EXPERIMENTS IN SOUND. . . .   Quill's
biting alto on *Omo* seemed hung up in the tempo, and he never
quite gets off the ground   BIRD FEATHERS Isn't it time these
experiments in necrolatry came to an end? If McLean, Jenkins,
Quill, and Woods have anything personal to say, Prestige is not
helping them *or* us to find out about it with packaging like this.
There are, undoubtedly, customers for a platter of leftovers from
sundry past ornithological sessions, but I wonder what this
music will mean to them after a few playings. Ironically, if these
altoists went for the *whole* Bird, they might come up with more
expressive individual voices   Stitt is by far the most
authoritative of the players who emulate Parker. . . . Phil
Woods, too, is closely associated with the memory of Bird, but
he has a brash, salty humour in his playing that is reminiscent of
the jumping altos of the forties. . . . Julian "Cannonball"
Adderley is probably the best known of the Birdmen. He plays
with great assurance and verve. . . . Art Pepper is far superior to
the other West-Coasters, including the rather anemic Bud Shank
and the chilly Lennie Niehaus. . . . Gene Quill also tends to be
somewhat uncontrolled, but he is capable of very fine playing

strictly ad lib NEW YORK . . . Warner Bros. has recorded a
12-man sax ensemble to be released as *Saxophones, Inc.*
Personnel on the disc: Coleman Hawkins, Zoot Sims, Al Cohn,

Seldon Powell, and George Auld, tenors; Hal McCusick, soprano; Herb Geller, Phil Woods, and Gene Quill, altos

Phys Ed

He liked basketball; the rhythm of it, the sound of the ball on the varnished floor, all the faking and even some flying and the swish of it going through the hoop. Coach said, "Too bad you're a senior," and Vic thought, yeah, too bad, too late, too soon. Needed a shower, felt good but sad.

Study Hall

Hall pass. Library.
BIG BIRD ORBITS WORDS A human voice, cradled in outer space, spoke a message. . . . "This is the President of the United States . . . my voice is coming to you from a satellite"
The engaging children of Communist China in the picture above are being firmly shaped to the service of what may one day be the mightiest nation on earth.   Smokey, who now lives in the Washington, D.C., zoo, was a real-life bear cub.   You've probably never heard of the Advertising Council   CASTRO IN TRIUMPHANT ADVANCE TO HAVANA   as firing squad bullets rip through him and send his hat flying   Stumblebum Hero Stars in "Maverick"   BLACK AFRICA SURGES TO INDEPENDENCE
This is the life for you in Florida Shores   John D. Rockefeller IV carefully deciphers gravestone in a Tokyo cemetery   PAT BOONE BOOM   It was budget time and the face of Lyndon Johnson was grim and skeptical. . . . powerful leader of the Democratic opposition, he had some hard questions. . . . Is the administration willing to spend enough in the face of Russia's missile advances?
Seventeen Negro students admitted to white schools in Norfolk   Rebounding skill depends mostly on timing and reach, but it also requires such semilegitimate acts   Disc

jockey's 201-hour stunt adds to scientific knowledge of sleeplessness   Builders like Mackles boost Florida Boom in housing for new settlers   If you project a line from the magic lantern to the "feelies" predicted in Aldous Huxley's *Brave New World* we are nearing the end. . . . What John Crosby calls TV's "creeping mediocrity" is even charged with brutalizing, cretinizing, or at best homogenizing our young. . . . The networks might correct this by taking all control away from advertisers, as is the practice in British commercial TV. The question could also be tested by really trying a system of pay-as-you-listen TV, with a view toward restoring the direct relation between entertainer and audience   THE LAST MOGUL: SAM GOLDWYN   DOLPHINS AND WHALES: FUNNIEST AND SMARTEST THINGS IN THE SEA   The Spell of Scott Fitzgerald Grows Stronger   OLD-STYLE MAFIA AND ITS HEIRS, THE CALCULATORS   EVER SINCE INCA TIMES, THE TRIBESMEN OF PERU HAVE WORN . . . U.S. Skiers have been snatching them up as fast as they are imported   Murrow, TV's star and top critic, takes year off   New York Says Tsk Tsk at African Attire   A cigar brings out the caveman in you   The sawing of hill-billy fiddles and the beat of rock and roll guitars has made many a deafened diner or drinker wish he could bribe the jukebox to be quiet. Now he can, thanks to. . . . SILENCE ON A PLATTER   U.S. STAYS UP TO VIEW PAAR   THE "CLAN" IS THE MOST Led by Sinatra and Martin, it hoots at Hollywood's names and old traditions   PHOTOGRAPHER RICHARD AVEDON FEELS THIS IS THE REAL MARILYN, A LOVING WIFE PLAYFULLY KISSING HER BRILLIANT HUSBAND, PLAYWRIGHT ARTHUR MILLER   Steve Allen made it big on television by inducing nationwide insomnia as master of ceremonies of the late night *Tonight* show. Moving to a prime and decent Sunday evening hour, he has won even more conspicuous success, thanks almost wholly to his own engaging personality   NEW STARS PAUL NEWMAN DEBBIE REYNOLDS Nick Adams Shirley MacLaine Don Murray Marge Champion Tommy Sands Sherrie North Rock Hudson Fess Parker Kim Novak Gower Champion

Buddy Ebsen Lee Remick Dana Wynter Jim Garner Joan
Collins   In Las Vegas, Paris imports who see nothing novel
in nudity   The young son of famous parents, Ricky Nelson
has become famous himself

Pignatari has earned the title of world's top playboy
Sinatra's nonconforming playmates   MacLeish's *J.B.*, which
likens modern man to Job, is called "one of the most memorable
works of the century"   Photodiagrams explain what makes
the stereo listener feel he is sitting in the middle of an
orchestra   The cult of rock 'n' roll, led by boyish idols
like Dick Clark (left) and deliriously joined by millions of
youngsters, makes an ever-noisier impact on the musical
scene   *The Diary of Ann Frank* is told in photographs taken
on the set and in Stevens's own words

How people all over react to one Sullivan show joke   As
unexpected guest of Georgia, diplomatic Negro has fine
time   Join this happy crowd. Look smart. Stay young and
fair and debonair. Be sociable. Have a Pepsi.

Lunch

Macaroni and cheese, spinach, coleslaw, peanut but-
ter cookies. Vic didn't smoke anymore, so he skipped the Edge. He
got enough smoke playing in clubs. It even bugged him when Baz
smoked in the funeral dorm. Maybe Baz was out there sharing his
screwdrivers with Junior Hazlewood and Mick Moran.

English

He'd already recited his prologue to Chaucer, so he
read while some others did theirs. Memorizing was no big deal to
somebody who read and played music, who'd memorized piano and
saxophone concerti for recitals, who could sing the lyrics to most
Broadway songs and knew most of a musician's fakebook by heart.
At the end of the period, he handed in his senior paper, "Nonconformity: The Prize and the Price—A Study of Individualism in

the Work of Joyce, Kerouac, Pasternak, and Salinger." He'd typed it carefully on the funeral home typewriter, and Mrs. Benoit seemed impressed.

Music Theory

Miss Cook tried to recruit him for choir and for the part of Joe in *Show Boat*. He pointed out that choir was in the same period as band, and she nodded as if she'd forgotten. "But you could still rehearse after school." He said he'd let her know.

Band

On the field, rehearsing for Gasparilla, the pirate parade in Tampa's version of Mardi Gras, next week. They'd all miss school for it. It was cold, and marching felt good, and he only remembered the hot weather when his shoes broke through the grass on a turn and that jungle smell came up from the wet earth.

Home

On duty. Took Mr. Fortunato home from his radiation treatments. Everyone knew they weren't working. His hair had fallen out and he was so light Vic could lift him to his bed alone—gently, because he knew that everything hurt this good man—and Mr. Fortunato gave him a dollar tip that his wife wouldn't take back later in the living room. Her eyes were large, luminous, but she'd already done most of her crying. Vic saw that Mr. Fortunato had held it crumpled in his hand all day just to give to him, and even now he wasn't calling for her, though Vic knew he needed another shot. Vic didn't know how to live with all the pain he was seeing, and soon he was supposed to be an adult.

He read *The Catcher in the Rye:* " 'This fall I think you're riding for—it's a special kind of fall, a horrible kind. The man falling isn't permitted to feel or hear himself hit bottom. He just keeps falling and falling. The whole arrangement's designed for men who, at some time or other in their lives, were looking for something their own environment couldn't supply them with. Or they thought their own environment couldn't supply them with. So they gave up looking. They gave it up before they even got started. You follow me?' . . .

"There were only about five or six other kids on the ride, and the song the carousel was playing was 'Smoke Gets in Your Eyes.' It was playing it very jazzy and funny. All the kids kept trying to grab for the gold ring, and so was old Phoebe, and I was sort of afraid she would fall off the goddamned horse, but I didn't say anything or do anything. The thing with kids is, if they want to grab for the gold ring, you have to let them do it, and not say anything. If they fall off, they fall off, but it's bad if you say anything to them."

Under the Double Eagle

It was a beautiful day for a parade. Tampa celebrated the invasion of the pirate José Gaspar with almost as much
abandon as the rest of the world celebrated Mardi Gras. Bankers and
lawyers painted scars on their faces and wore black eye patches and
pinched girls who would have slapped them any other day. Everybody was a pirate for a day, an invader, plunderer, freebooter.

Burdened with the season of grief at the funeral home, Vic and
Baz were looking for some abandon, too, so when the band bus
dropped them at the parade staging area on Franklin Street, which
was the wino district anyway, they slipped away to a dark bar where
men and women who drank every day grumbled about the amateurs
outside and the bartender didn't see anything untoward about selling
a few drinks to two men in uniform. They ordered rum and Coke.
Vic told the barflies that he and Baz were members of the Basque
government-in-exile color guard and jai alai team.

It was such a relief to be there in that loose time. Why, Vic wondered, doesn't our nation have more of these festivals? And if we knew we could celebrate together, getting high and loving whom we liked, wouldn't there be fewer of these poor veterans doing it all year long? Couldn't we have at least as much joy as we have grief? "We need a Get Drunk and Naked Day," he told an approving Basil Belheumer. A Let It All Hang Out Day. A White People's Saturday Night as good as the black people gave themselves most weeks. We could return Halloween to its ancient Druidic purposes and, instead of watching ads for candy on TV once a year, get out into a foggy forest and dance naked in the moonlight. "Now you're talkin'," the winos were saying, long past dancing themselves. No matter, Vic and Baz were having so much fun toasting José Gaspar and the New Halloween and Basque independence that by the time they got back to the band assembly point, the bus that still contained their instruments had already left to meet them at the parade's end. They hadn't wanted to carry their horns into the bar.

Now they were gone. He and Baz were soldiers without rifles, riders without horses, archers with no bows. Mr. Branthooven blew his whistle, began the series of short shrills that signaled the drummers to roll off for a cadence, then stopped. He walked through the ranks to Vic, who stood foolishly with his right arm in the carry position for an imaginary saxophone. Branthooven came up close, and his nose wrinkled. He went to inspect Baz. Then he returned and started the cadence, and the band stepped off. Within a block they began "Under the Double Eagle," Vic's favorite march. It was one of the most ridiculous, most impotent, saddest feelings he'd ever had, and it was one of the longest parades they did, winding through downtown Tampa along Bayshore Boulevard and past the Davis Island bridge. Every step was a humiliation. The bright sun mocked them. The one thing I know I can do, he thought, and I can't do it.

The pretty girl on the float ahead, bored finally with waving and being looked at, squinted in the sun at him and shrugged her shoulders as if to say, what gives? The rum wore off fast and left him with a mild headache and a dry mouth. The pirates walking alongside, drunk as rats in a mash barrel, kidded *him*. If someone threw a coin or pirate's trinket or spitball, it seemed to hit only him. Some kids who'd taken to running through the bands for laughs stopped and trailed along with him and jeered. "What are you, a singer?" they asked. "What a feeb." He tried to cheer himself by imagining that he'd reduced Tampa, Tamerlane style, to a great pile of skulls.

At the end of the parade, none of the other players seemed to see him. As the others scrambled for their instrument cases and seats on the bus, Mr. Branthooven told them both that they were expelled from the band. The dean would have to decide about the rest of school.

My Funny Valentine

He had to see Boop. He didn't know how to reach
Tonto or Buster, and he didn't want to ask them anyway. His only
chance was Chick Czement. The switchboard rang his room and he
answered.

"I need Betty Boop for a gig," Vic said. "But it's pretty confidential."

"I can dig that," Chick said.

"I mean really," Vic said. "You know how to reach her?"

A silence meant either that Chick was suspicious or that he was
looking for it. But he couldn't look for it. He was blind. "Listen," he
said finally. "Maybe you already know this, and maybe if you don't
I shouldn't get into it, but there are two numbers, really. Now you
gotta keep this between us. There's a number to call for singing gigs,
and for other gigs, too, if you know—"

"I know," Vic said. "Not that one. That's Ice."

"I'm hip," Chick said. "But she's trying to get out of that. She auditioned here. Waiting to hear if the boss has the balls to use a colored singer, but also, he's got another club in Jersey. So you call this other number. Her friend who doesn't work for Ice. And be careful. Ice is bad news."

"Solid. Read on."

"Read, that's a grin, man." Chick gave him a number. "But dig," Chick said, then paused. Finally he said, "You're a young cat. You should know that with Boop comes a habit. 'Course you're only looking to get her to sing, right? But just in case. I like you, man. You play good. Take care of your chops."

Vic thanked him and called the number and left a message with the friend, and an hour later Boop called him at the funeral home. "Man, you got to get *out* of there," she said. "That's too spooky. You know we can't be seein' each other."

"I gotta," he said. It was all he could think of. There was no argument for it. It made no sense for either of them. He didn't even know why he wanted it, but want it he did, and he didn't care at what price. Then he thought of that. "I'll pay you," he said.

There was a long silence. "Oh, you dumb-ass boy," she said finally, her voice weary.

"I just mean to cool Ice," he said.

"That *better* be what you meant. But you oughta know nothin' gonna cool Ice 'bout you now 'cept maybe cuttin' your thoat. He go beyond mean where you come in."

"I don't care," Vic said and let it ride with that.

Boop told him a hotel and a room number. It was on the north side, in the small black neighborhood around the gas plant, and it was the only place in that part of the state where a mixed couple might meet safely. Salt and pepper. Midnight, she said. Ice was delivering something. No car and no scooter. Cab to the white bar a block past the Sears store and walk the rest, fast and quiet. No front door. In the back and up the stairs to 203 and knock three times, then two more.

He parked the car in a metered space downtown and took a cab from there. If there was trouble he'd rather have it waiting a mile or so away. He knew now that he could run a mile if he had to.

"I work bar-back for this guy," he told the cabbie in front of the Detroit Bar. "He owes me some money. He can't say he doesn't have it this time of night."

"You should write a book," the cabbie said, and Vic felt like somebody in a private eye novel.

He walked fast and quietly and went up the back stairs. He was surprised at how clean the hotel was, and fairly quiet, though Monday was always a slow night. He knocked three times, then two, and nobody answered. He did it again. Then he tried the door. It opened into a dark room and he found a light switch. The room had only a battered dresser, a night table, and a bed. Boop was lying in the bed. Asleep? Drunk? Dead? He smelled smoke and saw an ashtray on the night table with a cigarette almost burned out. There was also a fifth of gin and a glass. He heard a kind of tingle in the air, faint alarm, growing. Maybe feelings come as sounds to musicians, to the mind's ear. He heard his breath and heart as he approached the bed, went quickly back to shut the door, returned to touch Boop.

She opened her eyes, and her pupils had consumed her irises. She sighed. "You lock the door?" she asked.

He went back and did. It was one of those old doors that locked with the same key outside or in. He knew she was high. He turned to see her eyes closed again, sheet pulled up to her chin like a patient in a hospital. "I wish you wouldn't shoot that stuff," he said. His voice sounded very young to him. He didn't see any works, but she was high. That gin wouldn't make her pupils open like some animal's in the dark.

She pulled the pillow from behind her head and held it over her face to show her irritation with him. The sheet slipped down to show breasts—which he hadn't seen in the car—like ripe tropical fruit. He'd like to feel their weight, nurse on them. He'd like to run home. He didn't know what to do. His mother had told him last year, after a psychology class brought it up, that she had tried to nurse him, but he'd been so greedy it made her nervous and her milk dried up. Now here was his white boy *National Geographic* fantasy in the flesh, right in his own hometown, in a bed, inches away. Maybe he could still just run out of the hotel and all the way to his car. What was this hunger, thirst, craving, and could he satisfy it here? Was it love, sex, defiance? Did anybody ever get enough? Did anybody ever understand it? Did you ever stop being afraid? She was humming something under the pillow.

She took the pillow off her face and held it over her breasts. "I only horned a little bit," she said. "You know, sniff? Snort? With a little coke, to stay wake. You think I don't know my business?"

"This isn't business," he said, his voice louder and really shaky.

"Turn out the light," she said.

"Why?"

"Because you can't tell the difference after dark."

Maybe he didn't want the light on, either. Maybe he didn't even want to be here. He walked over and turned out the light. Boop was humming something. He didn't recognize the tune.

She stopped humming. "Come on, Vic," she said in a lazy voice. "Come on over here, sweet boy."

So he did, shedding his clothes on the bare wood floor as he walked to her, and it was the second time he'd ever been in bed with a woman, and the sheets she opened for him let him in way over his head—suddenly, with the act of trusting his weight to that squeaky bed, changing his life way more than he thought he could handle.

Boop knew her business. Her mouth tasted of stale smoke and gin, but he was thirsty. He could smell her sweat with her perfume, but now he wanted to sweat, too. They wrapped around each other suddenly, both breathing quick, making little grunts of surprise and pleasure. He stopped, thinking of the rubber he'd bought. She stopped with him, waiting. "I oughta wear something," he said.

"Go get it. You got it with you?" She didn't seem to mind. She sang the song again in that broken little Lady Day voice. He found the thing in his wallet, fumbled with the wrapping, and when he had it out his erection was gone. His eyes were adjusting to the dark room now, and he figured she could see him even better with those black, dilated lemur eyes. She laughed. "Where's my man at?" she joked.

"Shit," he said.

"Come here," Boop said. "Stand by the bed and I'll find you in the dark with my mouth. Close your eyes. Have that skin ready."

Just the idea of it worked. He did close his eyes, heard the sheets rustle with her movement, felt her lips on his thigh, her tongue. He was so hard already that he wondered if he would feel her when she reached it. "Lot of black girls won't do this," she said, and he knew how close she was from the sound . . . to taking . . . him all in, all the way down to his groin, where she moved her head in half-circles, then coming back slowly, her tongue dragging along the bottom of it. Then another half-circle with her lips and tongue just over the tip, and down again. And he came. She held his testicles, not seeming surprised.

His body lost its rigidity, and all of him relaxed enough to be embarrassed. She pulled at him, situating them until he stood over her and she was comfortable with her head on a pillow. She just let his soft penis lie across her mouth as he stood beside the bed. She reached out lazily now and then with her tongue. When he was beginning to want it again, she turned her head and let him thrust it in, then pulled away, teasing him.

She put the rubber onto him. "Now," she said, rearranging herself on the bed. "You can give me a nice ride too. Come down on me, child."

She showed him what to do, and he played backup like in the Blue Room that afternoon, punching up her song, playing where she wasn't singing, near the end weaving their voices together in the out chorus. And giving each other a quieter applause—kisses, sighs, all the romantic stuff of the ballads, but this time with funk.

They lay side by side, her head in the crook of his right arm. She was smoking. He smelled his own sweat now, too. He wanted to say something about how he felt, but he figured it was only another chance to sound stupid. He wanted to put his mouth on her breasts, but it was too late and she'd make fun of it. She said, "I told you you got potential." He smiled in the dark. A little later she asked, "You gonna stay here all night?"

He felt his face blush with his quick shame. He hadn't expected that question and it stung. He hadn't planned to stay, but now he was angry. "Hell no, I'm splitting. Why, you need to fix?" What was wrong with him? "You got another date?"

She sat up, leaning on her extended left arm, breasts swinging just above him, her right fist clinched. "Who are you to ask me that? Are you Ice? Yeah, I want to fix."

"Me too," he said without thinking. He remembered the boy in

The Red Badge of Courage, watching men drop around him but willing himself to go on, walking to meet the Great Death so he could be a man. This was a different red badge, but it was still the Great Death.

She shifted her weight until her right palm was digging into his left hip and she was hanging over him, angry voice, soft breasts.

"Don't you *never* say that again," she said.

He felt stubborn, as with his parents, blind will in charge. "Who says I don't get to do what I want?" he asked. "I want to snort some. Why shouldn't I try?"

"Because the trying's too good," she said. "That fat, juicy worm be all the way in your stomach 'fore you feel the hook."

"I'd be a gentleman junkie, a chipper."

She let all her breath out angrily, rolling away from him to the edge of the bed.

"And I can get it anywhere, if I want it," he added.

"Why you want to hurt me?" she asked, her voice dull and distant.

He put his hand on her shoulder. "I wouldn't hurt you. Why would that hurt you?"

" 'Cause that's the one bad thing I ain't done. I been a junkie and a ho', but I never tried to push junk on nobody."

He didn't know anymore why he was pushing it. He wasn't even sure what he'd say next. His argument came out of a part of his mind he didn't know. "Maybe it's the thing that'll get me past the self-consciousness that's holding back my playing."

"Shit!" she said, rolling back over to face him, pulling the sheet up to cover her breasts. "I use junk. Billie Holiday uses junk. Do I sing as good as her? Is either one of us happy? That's what I thought, too. You want to be as good as Bird, and all you'll get is the chance to be as sick as Bird."

"Quill," he said.

"Junkie!" she shouted. "Your big hero. A junkie and a lush. I asked around."

He looked away. He wanted to hit her. He didn't believe her. Maybe he did believe her. Maybe he'd already heard that himself in that part of his mind that pushed him now. He didn't even want the stuff. He was terrified of it. He tried one more argument. "I thought we could do it together, just once. Then I'd know the score and I'd be satisfied."

She got up and went into the bathroom. He heard her crying, a sad, small voice. He got up and looked in. She was chopping at something with a razor blade on a compact mirror, making a powder. Then she put that aside. She put something onto a spoon and lit a match under it. Her back obscured his view. She was still crying. "Go get a dollar bill," she said. "Roll it tight like a tube." He knew he should stop it here—he was hurting her—but he went and did it. When he came back she was sitting on the toilet, her left arm tied off with a bathrobe belt. The empty spoon was in the sink. The needle was in a vein on her wrist, the eyedropper already squeezed through the little paper adapter sleeve Baz had described to him. Blood was creeping up into the dropper, staining the paper. She squeezed it back but still didn't take the needle out. "Snort that on the mirror," she said. "Welcome to the life."

Her eyes were closed, her face gray, her body sagging. A small smile came to her face. "Don't you want to take it out?" he asked.

"Just like a man," she said, laughing giddily with maybe a touch of cruelty. "Want to take it out too soon. What you waitin' for boy? You can be the next genius."

He sucked most of the powder into his right nostril, sneezed, got himself under control, and finished it in the left. She took out the spike and held some toilet paper hard over the spot to stop the bleeding. He pulled her up and they went to bed.

She hummed next to his ear. She smoked but dropped the cigarette beside the bed, and he had to get up and put it out. He didn't feel much at first. What was all the fuss about? Then he thought he felt a lurch of relaxation, like slipping further into a hot bathtub. Along the backs of his arms and legs and across his scalp and forehead, as Baz had described it from his own one time with his dad's stash. He felt well, whole. Lying in this cheap room with a black junkie whore, he felt perfect and loving and fell asleep.

In the first morning light he smelled the ashtray and heard Boop snoring. He opened his eyes and looked at her. She was lying on her side facing him. The hair along the edge of her forehead and temples was crinkly and brittle-looking, and she had a shadow of a sideburn along her cheek. There was a crust at the corners of her mouth and her breath was sour on him. He got up and dressed, tossed cold water onto his face, and did what he could with his hair. He was going to look strange enough walking the early morning streets in this part of town.

Blame It on My Youth

Home Room

Called to Dean's Office. His decision was that Vic and Baz were on probation. Miss Cook had interceded for both of them and they would be probationary members of the choir. Miss Cook came in, scowling at them appropriately. "You're going to be my Joe," she told Vic.

"Yes, ma'am," he said.

"And you, Mr. Belheumer, are one of the slaves in the chorus. One screwup and I tell the dean and you will not be graduated."

"Yes ma'am," Baz said.

"See you fifth and sixth periods," she said. "Rehearsal's tonight at seven. Don't eat a heavy supper." Vic started to say something about work, and her eyes told him to let it go. It would be easier to get Doug to cover in this postseason decline in the funereal business cycle than to deal with Miss Cook. It would probably be easier right now to get people to stop dying than to deal with Miss Cook.

Art

Emily gave him a note that read: "I'm pregnant." As he sat behind his drawing table, the open note and an unopened *Down Beat* before him, trying to figure out how somebody could get all the blues at once, a kid came with another note for him to see the dean. Vic said he'd already been, but the little jerk junior said, "I *know* that. He wants you a*gain*."

In the Dean's Office were Dean Batten, Officer Crump, and the cotillion girl. She didn't need a note. It was obvious that she was pregnant. Crump looked smug instead of angry. The dean introduced the girl as Crump's niece. Vic heard the voice as if at a great distance, but he heard his pulse thundering in his temples, his neck, maybe in his brain. His body felt cold, and he didn't think he could move. Maybe he'd faint, or maybe this was a heart attack coming on and it would save him.

"You understand that I have no authority in this matter," the dean told him, "but in view of other recent events, this looks pretty bad for you." The meeting ended with neither Crump nor the girl nor Vic having said a word. Vic felt he was staggering on the way back to art class. What was he supposed to do? He'd been careful, even with Boop. Boop reminded him of the blues. Staggering under the sheer weight of trouble, there in the prime of his innocent/corrupt youth in his white high school, he tried to think of a lyric that would soothe him. "I'd rather drink muddy water and sleep in a hollow log" was all he could come up with.

He rounded a corner and ran into Miss Cook again. "You look pale," she said, and he blurted it all out, right there in the hallway. She listened with only a mild frown, then said, "If you're telling me the truth, I don't think you have to do anything. Morally, I mean. Women are responsible for their bodies. If you did your part, let it go. We've got a show to put on."

He said, "What?"

"I said we've got a show to do. Quit whining. Grow up."

"I don't want to grow up," he said.

"I don't blame you." She actually smiled. "I don't blame you. Give me a call if it gets too bad, but you be there at seven tonight, sharp."

"Yes, ma'am."

Phys Ed

Boxing, the coach believing that even the palest of bookworms should know the rudiments of the manly art of self-defense. After the demo (Vic had learned all that from his father years ago) they paired off. Jimmy Johanssen picked him, thinking they'd help each other skate. Then Jimmy started goofing around with his crazy, quick hands, jabbing Vic in the face and making noises like a fight in a western serial. After some glove leather caught his open eye on about the fourth of Jimmy's jabs, Vic lost himself in a red rage, all of it coming out at once on this innocent target, and didn't stop until he had Jimmy on his back and was ripping at his own gloves so as to get them off and hit him with his bare fists. Jimmy was making his stepped-on puppy noise, and perhaps it was the sheer silliness of that and not the coach's force that cooled Vic. He was sure this would be the end, his last Dean's Office visit, but the coach seemed to think the whole thing was just a matter of in-appropriate gusto, too much of a good thing, and Jimmy didn't want to push it.

Shower. Vic stood as long as he thought he could, letting the warm water sting his neck and back.

Study Hall

Hall pass. Library.

A PISTOL-PACKING NYASALAND MAMA In troubled Nyasaland, Mrs. Joyce Ness, taking her daughter for a walk on her husband's tea plantation, carries a loaded Colt .45 at her hip and took a police dog along for protection. Although no whites have been slain   fed up with the singing chipmunk

   The Pros and Cons of Island Statehood   A Mighty Glue—
Epoxy   RED SPIES' VIENNA HANGOUTS   Yale

undergraduates have a tradition of skirmishes with local cops and "townies"   AN IROQUOIS WAR ON WHITE MAN'S LAND   TIBET TAKES ON RED CHINA   TWO-WAY CRAM is tried by phone-boothers   PROMISING ATTACK IN CANCER BATTLE   Orson Welles, as Darrow, defends Leopold, Loeb   Billy Wilder shows Marilyn how to swish through steam of train coach   Bigtime Politics in High School   The front-running candidate for the 1960 presidential nomination, Senator John F. Kennedy, has just met a couple of the most critical tests of the young campaign   The peekaboo style, as taught by Patterson's garrulous manager, Cus d'Amato, is a radical departure from the classic stance of John L. Sullivan   Answer: Budweiser . . . *King* of Beers

Life: AMERICA'S OWN MUSIC IN ITS LUSTY YOUTH. JAZZ Spawned in New Orleans cemeteries and saloons, it went north by riverboat

Trouble in mind, I'm blue. But I won't be blue always.
'Cause the sun's gonna shine in my back door someday.

From an unpainted back step, a broken hay rake, a stump by the dusty road, the solitary Negro singers raised their song. The song was the blues. Though it sang of bad times it sang vigorously, looking to the day when good times would come. And it was this hopefulness that kept the blues from vanishing in the stillness of the South's back country. Persisting through the post–Civil War years, the songs passed from singer to singer. They became in time the tap root of the completely original art form called jazz, which captivated the world and became America's favorite musical entertainment. . . . *The Funky Butt Hall, that place was wild as pig's knuckles. And they had all kinds of coon shouters. A coon shouter was mostly the ones that used to sing the blues. . . . Lot of them died, and a lot of them went away. . . . And in Storyville you had anything you want. Beautiful women, man. For years you couldn't get a band out of New Orleans because it was just too great. . . .* In 1917 the ax fell on New Orleans jazz when the Secretary of the Navy closed Storyville as a menace to the fleet. Disconsolate at having to leave their good times behind, the New Orleans jazzmen found an avenue of escape up the Mississippi. . . . mainly in Chicago—just in time to provide the music most suitable to the wild days of prohibition and gangsters. *Sometimes Capone's gang would come in, have a good time, put their guns on the table. There wasn't no trouble. Those gangsters all liked jazz. Used to bring us liquor.*

Vic felt a little better.

Lunch

Spaghetti again. Yes. He knew he felt better, and it was hanging with him. Something about being so bad there was no point fighting it. Something about surrender, about singing in your chains. Maybe they'd have understood at the Funky Butt Hall. Baz offered him some screwdriver but he passed.

English

Mrs. Benoit returned their senior papers. Vic got an A+, and she seemed almost on the verge of tears as she handed it back. What a strange day this had been, and not close to being over yet.

Music Theory

Final exams back. Vic got a B+. Class converted to a rehearsal for *Show Boat*. To auditorium. Miss Cook gave him the score. "Learn your part."

Choir

Same. Rehearsal for *Show Boat*. "We will *not* sing 'Niggers all work on the Mississippi' in the introduction to Joe's 'Old Man River' solo. We will sing 'Po folks all work on the Mississippi.'" A few giggles, quickly and ruthlessly suppressed by Miss Cook. "I won't *have* it," she said, and he wondered if they knew exactly what she meant. He wondered if he did. Was he really going to put on blackface and walk out there alone and sing "Old Man River" like somebody who'd toted barges, lifted bales? Well, he'd gotten a little drunk and he'd landed in jail, and if they were going to find anybody in this school who'd had the blues, he was probably it this season. So what the hell, it was this or no diploma.

Home

Doug agreed to cover for them at the funeral home as long as he could. Maybe he could get his nephew to come in. Did he actually say "The show must go on"? Rehearsal, in the auditorium, seven to nearly midnight. "Tote that barge, lift that bale."

Old Man River

His father checked out a Riggins Brothers demonstrator for the performance. Then, for insurance, he removed even its drab hubcaps.

Miss Cook was apparently a publicity genius, too, and advance ticket sales for *Show Boat* suggested, demanded, a three-night run. They had rehearsed every night for three weeks, blocking it out, choreographing the rudimentary dance numbers, coordinating the chorus and solo work, the lights, the small professional white orchestra from the union local that had donated its time but was getting cranky by dress rehearsal along with everybody else. Even the mayor and local congressman had bought tickets, and such was Miss Cook's power that they would actually come. His Aunt Glad and Uncle Homer were there. He'd told the cats in Buster's combo one Saturday night that he was being forced to sing the Joe part. As he'd feared, Miss Cook's publicity had reached them, too, and they just nodded coolly, ironic and distant behind lidded eyes.

Vic was not yet, might never be, a bass with the full deep range of Paul Robeson, Jules Bledsoe, or William Warfield, so his solo was raised to a higher key, the musicians transposing or rewriting their scores. The dress rehearsal had gone pretty well, kids in the slave gang giggling briefly about their blackface makeup but never within reach of Miss Cook, whose theory of leadership, like Genghis Khan's and Tamerlane's, was to make your troops more afraid of you than of the enemy, which in this case was the audience or the lurking backstage ghost of stage fright. She was a tiny but awesome presence everywhere, and even the union pros sat up straight when, forgetting their volunteer status, she told them to.

Funeral Doug seemed to be getting by all right with his nephew and his nephew's friend—a pair of wet smacks in their mid-twenties who probably were born for the business and now had an opportunity to realize it, might even catch hold enough to move out of their parents' houses and into the dorm above the prep room. Doug, in fact, had tickets to the show. It did seem that even the dying were afraid to interfere with Miss Cook's plans for a hit. Vic heard that Emily Dickinson had patched things up with Billy Glover and they would be married in June.

Vic loved the whole thing. He loved the Jerome Kern music, the Hammerstein lyrics (*"Why do I love you? Why do you love me? Why should there be two, happy as we?"*). He loved the idea of Tim Twitty, whose claim to fame until now was having been arrested by Crump for peeking into Claudia Dejeuner's bedroom window, stepping forward in blackface to say, "Ribber boat's a-comin'!" It was much better than Danny Sheehan's children's productions because here they had the real—actually, the exaggerated—emotions of adolescents. Backstage tantrums, feuds, and romances burst into flame briefly, only to be smothered by Miss Cook's dire will. Baz in blackface looked like a Lebanese rug merchant who'd been slipped a mickey by ruthless competitors, painted like a minstrel, and sold unconscious to slave traders.

Vic knew he was lucky to have this show to divert him from the truth that his life was falling apart. He assumed that Branthooven would nix the Juilliard audition and even the band scholarships, and he knew he'd never make it as a singer, but there was no time to think about that. When Baz asked him what he thought would happen with their scholarships, Vic said maybe they could learn some rock and roll guitar.

On opening night the momentum of the three weeks seemed to propel them through the first curtain and beyond any anxiety they might have had to get the show, as Vic's dad might say, on the road. Miss Cook's presence was everywhere, though she had now taken her performance station in the prompter's box cum conductor's blind between the stage and the orchestra. Vic thought it was uncanny how the sheer force of her personality seemed to move them to act almost like professionals. If he'd been asked to describe how her presence was felt, he'd have said he could hear her will ticking, like a metronome, or maybe like a bomb.

No bomb. The performance quickly found its own life, and awkward, adenoidal adolescents coalesced into a troupe. Vic was able to enjoy it because there wasn't much to worry about in his part until his solo, sung in act I, scene 1, and reprised in act II, scene 7. But as that first time drew near, as the blackfaced teenage slaves gathered round him for "Old Man River," there came a commotion in the rear of the auditorium, something powerful enough to overcome even Miss Cook's iron will.

It was difficult to see from the stage, with the lights in their eyes, and Miss Cook had no view of it at all. The ushers were arguing with people who had just come in, people who wanted seats where there were none and who, when told that, said they'd watch from standing room. But the ushers didn't know what to do about that request, because it wasn't from ordinary proud (or maybe even a little drunk) parents straggling in late from a restaurant like New Yorkers, but from, as the phrase made its way by whispers down to the stage, a group of "real niggers."

Vic had just taken center stage. He stood in blackface, both in the physical spotlight and in the full light of irony. It seemed to fall to him, by virtue of this play they were doing, this script, this willing suspension of disbelief about who really ran things, to deal with this. They had just been singing "Po folks all work on the Mississippi," and now here were Negroes who weren't even happy with that. And it was, he realized even more fully in the weighty seconds that passed in the spotlight, actually up to him. He looked down at Miss Cook in the prompter's box and she nodded, and he thought he knew what she meant, hoped to God he knew what she meant, because he was going to do it anyway. "Brothers and sisters," Vic cried out in Joe's voice. "Come on down here. There's always room in the entertainment business for a *few* Negroes."

It was a measure of Miss Cook's control that while the audience buzzed as the late arrivals made their way to the stage, the cast did not. Vic watched the visitors find their way between the front row and orchestra, locate the steps at stage left, then come, one by one, joining their blackface brethren, into the light. Vic didn't recognize the three women or one of the men, but he knew Tonto, and he knew Buster.

Vic looked down into the prompter's booth and saw Miss Cook smiling, nodding at him to continue as the pretend Negroes opened their ranks to the real ones, and it came his time to sing a song of anger, consolation, hope—a version of the blues with people from whom and with whom he had only just begun his own lessons. Only Miss Cook's face, shining in the stagelights, made it possible.

> There's an old man called the Mississippi.
> That's the old man that I'd like to be.
> What does he care if the world's got troubles?
> What does he care if the land ain't free?

He heard the chorus, but he heard the new voices, too, richer, bolder, one of the women doing a little gospel lick. He heard Tonto say "Sing it," and so he did.

> Old Man River, that Old Man River.
> He must know somethin', but he don't say nothin'.
> That Old Man River, he keeps on rollin' along.
> He don't plant taters, he don't plant cotton,
> And them that plants 'em is soon forgotten.
> That Old Man River, he just keeps rollin' along.
> You and me, we sweat and strain, body all achin' and
>   racked with pain.
> Tote that barge, lift that bale.
> You gets a little drunk and you lands in jail.

The new voices behind him made him feel as Boop's hand had in the Blue Room, but there was more going on now. He couldn't explain it. Nobody in the audience was able to describe it later. In fact, nobody was really willing to talk about it to the reporters who asked them. The Negroes who had joined the cast stayed on stage all through the production, not so much participating (though neither did they interfere with the production) as looking on as social observers, giving the audience some reality to compare with the fantasy before them.

They joined in again on the reprise of "Old Man River."

Let me go 'way from this Mississippi.
Let me go 'way from the white man boss.
Show me that stream called the River Jordan.
That's the old stream that I longs to cross.

. . . .

I gets weary, and sick of tryin'.
I'm tired of living, but I'm scared of dyin',
That Old Man River, he just keeps rollin' along.

It worked. For a few minutes all wounds were healed, all grief comforted, all enmities buried. For a few minutes, everybody sang one song and mercy rained down—on the town, the school, the auditorium, the cast, the audience, and even on his Aunt Glad and Uncle Homer. Or so it seemed to Vic.

Round Midnight

He left a message with Boop's friend. Then, an hour later, he left another one. The woman sounded cautious, suspicious. Finally Boop called him back. "I can't see you. I heard you sang some soul, though."

"You gotta see me," he said. "I'm going nuts."

"I can't," she said.

He had to see her. He felt the iron force of *his* will—like Temujin, Genghis Khan, the prince named for iron. "Should I call Ice and make arrangements?" he asked. He couldn't believe he'd said it, but he wasn't backing off.

There was a short silence, then her weary voice. "Only deal Ice want to make with you is cuttin' your throat. Now he thinks you bein' treated like some white hero to the colored race. He crazy. You crazy too."

"Same time and place," he said and hung up when she didn't answer. Where was this ruthlessness coming from, this mean hunger? He didn't want to use junk again, he was sure, but then, he had been sure of that the first time.

Boop was in the bed as before, but she'd already fixed. A cigarette had burned itself up utterly, a long, gray caterpillar shape in the ashtray. Gin bottle half empty. Works and spoon on the same table. He touched her arm. Warm enough. Her face was swollen now and almost ashen, not sweated in anxiety but fading away from natural color somehow. What had been a handbag strap lay on the floor beside the bed. He knew it was a tourniquet. She opened her puffy eyes, shook her head vaguely. "Wha' you doin' here?" she asked.

He rubbed her arm foolishly as if that would speed the heroin along, bring her back to where she could remember. There was powder caked on her neck, and he remembered Baz telling him that junkies didn't bathe much because they couldn't stand the touch of water on their skin. "Stoned again," he said.

She smiled vaguely at her foolish boy, shook her head in friendly puzzlement. "Who's talkin'? Lil gentleman junkie. I come back and haunt you if you use this shit, I swear I will."

He just sat on the bed. After a while she said, "Take off your clothes and get in here. You want to see me, take a lil ride, you might as well take it. Can't hurt me none, but I may not . . . 'cause, you see . . . I'm a little high."

Her purse, heavy with something, was on the night table. The open closet was empty. He heard his blood coursing, a faint sound in his head, like electricity through a wire.

And then Ice, suddenly in the room through the door Vic hadn't locked, raised up like some black snake, reaching inside his coat for the sting. "Elvis!" he said. "I *cut* you!" Vic jumped onto the bed, stood in unbalanced confusion for a moment, wobbling at Boop's feet as if he might somehow protect her that way when it was Vic Ice would cut. Then, still confused, he used the bed's springs to launch himself not toward the closet or bathroom, where maybe he could barricade himself or at least postpone death, but toward Ice.

Vic's legs clamped around Ice's left side. He hooked his left arm under Ice's throat and reached his right behind Ice's shiny hair to grab the deadly right arm as it came out and raised up the razor. Vic grabbed his own right bicep with his left hand, locking his arms around Ice's neck. His legs around Ice's waist in a wrestler's scissor hold gave him some leverage to hold back that terrible arm. But he had no control of where Ice's legs took him, and so, locked together, they careened around the room, bouncing off walls and the dresser, tripping and almost falling over the foot of Boop's bed. Ice's left hand clawed at Vic's back, reached to pull at his hair and scratch his neck, but couldn't reach his eyes to do serious harm. Vic hoped Ice didn't lose his footing because he didn't know what he'd do with him on the ground.

Staggering around with Ice, Vic thought: This is all I know. Hold on. And think of something weird. What could be weird to Ice, who was a kind of walking, talking death? A sharp, fierce smell that Vic didn't recognize came up from Ice, overpowering the cologne, smoke, hair processor, gin. Then another thought came. As long as he tried to keep Ice from moving his hand forward, Ice struggled to do just that. What Ice really should do was go with Vic's force and take the razor back behind and cut Vic right off his back. Vic would have little strength or leverage pushing forward, so if Ice suddenly realized that that was the deadly direction, Vic probably couldn't stop him. But they were so closely intertwined that to Ice it might feel like cutting himself, and there was a chance he could do that.

Vic pulled back on the wrist fiercely, fearing the slickness of the sweat his fingers gripped now, wondering how long this could go on, looming around the room like some composite black/white Frankenstein monster, all attention on the razor that the cutter was trying to move in the wrong direction because, and only because, the white boy didn't seem to want to let him do that.

That was all he thought about. He heard nothing from Boop and saw very little as they reeled. His eyes stayed on the razor he was just able to see across Ice's shining hair. He saw some gray in that hair, and he was surprised to have found the limit of Ice's strength here. At one point Ice's eyes met his, just a few inches apart, and the two pairs of eyes told each other all the hate and fear in the world in a heartbeat, and beyond that a kind of regret. It's true, Vic almost thought (it all happened so fast), that it happens fast but you experience it slower. There's a kind of bond when you get this far, a warrior's love.

"Stop!" Boop was standing on the bed, unsteady, her legs pumping to try to keep her balance, holding a shaking pistol. From her handbag? It's a revolver, Vic thought. He could see the tips of several bullets in the cylinder that turned, slowly, in Boop's weak grip. He looked up at Boop's face. She was crying. Was she looking at Ice? Was she looking at him? Yes, she was looking at him, her pupils enormous. Aiming at him? He watched her close her eyes, and he heard the explosion later, after he and Ice had been thrown back, locked together, blinded by blood, against the wall, sagging down, together. Who was hit? God, the sudden coppery smell— Jesus, it was pumping!—how could he still be alive with this *blood* everywhere, his blood?

No, Ice's. The life left Ice suddenly, like a brief shiver, but the blood kept pumping for a time from his broken head, the right artery at his temple shot away with that part of his skull, just inches from Vic's face. Ice's blood still blinded him. He felt some pain begin now and wondered if the bullet had come through and hit him, too. He thought he had bone fragments in the skin of his face. Ice's body felt as small and weak as Mr. Fortunato's.

He began to try to push Ice's body off him. Boop was sitting on the bed now, the revolver hanging in her limp hand, like the woman outside Wolfie's. But this revolver had worked.

"Run, go, get out!" Boop said, not looking at him. Her voice was flat but urgent. Maybe she'd rehearsed this a lot of ways, and this was the way it would finally play—her show. "Don't say nothin'," she said. "Ever. Split. Keep runnin'. Don't look back."

Spring Can

Really Hang

You Up the Most

Juilliard was expecting him. He'd thrown his
bloody clothes into the crematorium and burned them, then washed,
sobbing, lucky Baz was out on a call. He'd dressed, gone down to
clean the car, burned those rags, too, and then lain awake in his
cot all night, waiting for the knock, the call. And in the morning
his mother called to say that Juilliard had phoned long distance to
confirm his audition, and he was to leave at seven that night, and his
dad said maybe he'd better come home anyway. All is forgiven.

He drove home with his clothes and horn and other things. Baz
had come in during the night and was asleep, so Vic left a note for
him and Doug. He was at home packing, still with that singing in his
head, when his mother called him to the phone. "It's Buster," she
said, "from *Show Boat*." As if it were the most natural thing in the
world. Maybe she thought Buster was a kid still pretending to be a
Negro. Maybe she was smarter than he thought.

"Your momma told me you're goin' up to try out," Buster said. "We straight with each other, right?"

"Yes," Vic said.

"I think you might as well go. You're good, and you might as well get a break. Boop says she wants you to go."

"Where is she?"

"In jail. They wouldn't let her see me, but we got her a lawyer and he told me, in code, dig? She said, 'Tell that young bird to fly.'"

"What'll happen to her?"

"Straight talk. She'll go from jail to prison. She got a big habit, and they won't cut her no slack there for it. That's unless somebody knows a good reason why she killed her pimp, her pusher. That way she goes to Lexington to kick. She might make that scene."

Vic thought about it for a short space. It was like listening to music, but he didn't know what music it was. It was powerful but stately. It was like a march to a very deadly war for a very important cause. Vic asked: "Who do I see?"

"You should think it out before you go," Buster warned. "Maybe you can reschedule up there. If you call the people. It's going to mean a world of trouble for you."

"I can't reschedule," Vic said. "They have too many people to hear. Maybe next year."

"You could go up and then go in when you get back," Buster said.

"But she'll be cold turkey, won't she, and they won't help her?"

"Yeah, and they might let her do it in the hospital if she's cleared. But listen, man, she's the junkie. You didn't make her be a junkie, and it ain't your problem now."

"I couldn't play for shit up there," he said. "I mean I can't even think straight." But he thought he knew how he felt, and that was that he didn't want to go to Juilliard, ever, never mind next year, never mind maybe. It really had little to do with Boop being in jail or hospital. He didn't think—well, he probably wasn't thinking straight—but he didn't feel he wanted to go at all. "I'll go down to the station now."

"You all right, Victor," Buster said, and maybe that was better than Juilliard. Buster gave him the lawyer's name.

It was a big story. When he got back from the police station and started to pack, his mother said, "Basil called. He said he's sorry, but they got somebody for your job. He said he's quitting, too."

"I don't know where to go," Vic said.

"This is your home," his mother said. "We're your family."

"You know what I did. It was true what they're saying on the radio, what'll be in the papers."

She shook her head, and he didn't know what that meant. "I'll fix you something to eat," she said.

Officer Krupke

Vic was drunk, in the Olds, alone, at the gangster's ghost house. He'd thrown his empties all over the sandspur and oyster-shell lot. He didn't care. He'd drunk almost a pint of bourbon and two six-packs of beer, and he had no Listerine. If he had, he thought, maybe he'd drink that, too.

He wasn't really surprised to see the patrol car, but he wondered if Crump's flashing light was broken. Crump came up in his usual slow "Gunsmoke" style, and after a while he ambled over to the car window and began to speak. Vic threw an empty beer can out, bouncing it off his shirt front. "You're a useless hump, Crump. You spend your life hanging around waiting for kids to fuck up. Why don't you go catch a real crook? Why don't you go fuck yourself?"

It took a while for that to register. Vic was surprised by it himself. "Why you little cocksucker," Crump said, his voice shaky with rage. "At least I'm not a nigger humper."

"You ain't qualified," Vic said. "You probably bang your niece instead." He went limp when Crump opened the door and dragged him out. He gave him dead weight to lift onto the hood, on his back, legs hanging over the fender well, dangling before the whitewalls and moon disks. Vic let his head rest uncomfortably on the hood louvers. Fuck this bastard.

Crump hit him in the ribs with the nightstick. He tried to sit up. Crump shoved him back and hit him with the nightstick in the ribs on the other side. "How's that feel?" he asked.

Vic didn't feel it much yet, except he couldn't breathe. He realized that he'd figured this all wrong, and he was more afraid than he'd ever been in his life, even with Ice. He'd thought that, having survived Ice, he couldn't be hurt by a cop, a guy himself accountable to the law. He had no time to wonder further. Crump leaned out with the nightstick and hit him precisely across his mouth. He tasted blood and knew a tooth was broken, maybe more. It hurt only in a vague, deep way now, signals trying to get through shocked tissue to sound the alarm. Vic heard Crump's leather gunbelt squeaking as he manuevered for just the blows he wanted. This was no indiscriminate beating.

Crump yanked Vic off the hood and hit him with a roundhouse right at the left point of his jaw. Vic let his head lie on his right arm across the fender until Crump yanked it up. "I'm wearing gloves," Crump said. "That felt good." Vic thought his jaw was broken. A pain shot up into his head, arcing across his forehead. A world of trouble, Buster had said.

Crump turned him around so he was facedown across the fender and hood this time, his broken face bleeding through the louvers and onto the air filter beneath. Vic began chanting to himself: "When that Aprill with his shoures soote." Crump struck one of his hands with the nightstick, and Vic heard cartilage and bone break long before he would feel it. "The Droghte of March hath perced to the roote." Crump hit the other hand. Vic saw his blood spreading on the hood near his face in the light of the new moon. "And bathed every veyne in swich licour." Half a tooth fell out. "Of which vertu engendred is the flour." Crump hit him across his kidneys.

He waited. He heard Crump walk away, boots crunching in the oyster shell. The pain began to build and kept on building. Crump started the police car and backed into a turn. More than he could ever have expected, the pain. He lost the sound of the cop car as he fainted and fell by the Olds.

But Not for Me

He went home after four days in the hospital.
He hadn't been lying out there long at the gangster's house before
another cruiser came by. Crump probably got scared. An anonymous
caller had reported a gang fight between blacks and whites, but the
patrolmen found only Vic lying there. Vic didn't say anything about
what had happened until he could talk to his father, and his father
said there'd been enough publicity already and not to mention it. The
doctors couldn't say whether he could play again. They said maybe.
The jaw was only dislocated, and he would drink his meals through
a straw for several days. The teeth could be replaced, though the
embouchure would feel strange. The hands were the tricky part. The
hospital had called in a specialist, and he'd done some surgery and
bandaged them. Boop was safe at Lexington.

Baz came by. He was staying temporarily with his dad and desperate for bread and someplace to go. He'd not gotten his scholarships
because of sheer competition, mostly from squares like Hathaway.

How could Vic expect to get one with a race-sex-drug murder scandal hanging over him and serious doubts about whether he'd ever play again?

Other people came by. It surprised him who did and who didn't. Aunt Glad and Uncle Homer were there. Blood was stronger than scandal. Uncle Homer asked some cagey questions. Then Vic heard him talking with his dad, but not what they were saying. Little Kingman came every day, and his mother most days, too, but never Big Kingman. Many of the band kids came by, and even Emily, to show him her ring. He felt like a broken war hero except he was . . . he was wondering what he could call it when Miss Cook came into his room. "What name would you give what I've become?" he asked her.

"Rogue and peasant slave is, I think, the correct term," she said. "Now cheer up and get well. A few people like you anyway." She started to leave, then came back. "I've got to say this. You've taken some stupid risks. It's gotten past the point of using inexperience as an excuse, or charming your way out of it. I'm really angry with you. You're a cat who's already used up some of his nine lives. I'd be afraid to know how many you've got left. Get well, but more important, get smart." His sister told him Miss Cook had been wiping her eyes as she left, but it still stung.

He could walk, though his taped ribs hurt. He watched TV with his dad. Steve Allen, Syd Caesar, a Jonathan Winters guest spot, "Maverick." It hurt to laugh, but he needed it even so. His dad had bought a "color conversion kit," a plastic screen to tape over the black-and-white TV. The screen was green on the bottom, pink in the middle, and blue at the top, and you watched your old black-and-white shows through it. There was a show coming next year called "The Twilight Zone," and he'd probably be right here to watch it— becoming a wet smack himself who lived with his folks and watched TV and had hobbies. On the news, Cronkite said two American military advisers had been killed in Vietnam while watching a Jeanne Crain movie in a tent. They were the first U.S. casualties in that conflict. Vic asked his father where Vietnam was, and his father said, "I don't know. Over there near Korea someplace. I'll tell you one thing, though. It'll never match the Civil War. More casualties than all our other wars put together."

"That's so long ago," Vic said, wondering how they could have killed so many without the atom bomb.

His father, a Civil War buff, looked sad. "The last Civil War veteran died this same week," he said. "I used to listen to them talk on the courthouse steps in Towanda. They were real people. They were twelve years old, some of them, when they went into battle. Boys your age were officers. This is a young country, like you. Neither one of you knows what the fuck you're doing."

Then one night after they'd all gone to bed, his mother called him to the phone. She had a look on her face that scared him. "It's a nurse," she whispered, and pointed north.

"Is this Mr. Victor Messenger?" the woman's voice asked, and he said yes. The singing noise was back, or maybe it was on the phone wires.

"I'm Nurse Fontanesi at the federal hospital in Lexington, Kentucky," she said.

He waited.

"I hope I'm not wrong about this. I have you listed as next of kin to a patient here named Elizabeth Burden. I only had the name, and this is the only Messenger in the book."

It was a mistake, he thought. A coincidence that Boop was there, too, some kind of clerical error. Then he knew better. "What's happened?" he asked. His voice must have sounded strange to the nurse—the jaw still painful to move and the front teeth gone.

"Are you the right person? I mean are you related—"

"She's a singer?"

"Yes, she was."

He waited. He felt his mother's arms around his waist—how long since she'd touched him?

"She died tonight, of natural causes."

"Natural?" His voice was a croak now. He wouldn't be able to talk again.

"Her heart. It happens. Maybe it will be some small comfort to know that she died clean."

"*Clean?*"

"I mean free of her addiction."

He dropped the receiver and it swung against the desk. Free of her addiction. That was it, all right. He felt his mother's arms tighten. His father and sister were in the room. The phone stopped hitting the desk and a tone like death droned from it. Lexington was off. He was surprised to learn that the sound of grief for him was a concert A above middle C. His pitch was not always perfect, but he knew this one.

Much later that morning, still unable to sleep, he read, in *The March of the Barbarians:* "They say: 'When that which is harder than a rock and stronger than the storm wind shall fail, the empires of the North Court and the South shall cease to be. When the White Tsar is no more, and the Son of Heaven has vanished, then the campfires of Genghis-Khan will be seen again, and his empire will stretch over the earth.' "

God Bless the Child

· beating—3 A.M. to be precise—when the noises began at Crump's
bedroom window. Crump, a bachelor, had gotten off work at midnight as usual and had gone right to bed, and to sleep.

Now there were rocks hitting his window. It wasn't hail. The
Murphys' dog was barking, but that damned dog barked at anything.
His bedroom was in the front of the house, just off the living room
and front door, and he could look out the window at his front yard.
Just as he did, another pebble hit the glass. The moonlight lit the
yard fairly well, but one patch was lighted with a flashlight, shining
up between a man's legs. The man was bent over, showing Crump
his bare ass and his darkly shaded hairy balls. There was no noise
associated with this strange assault beyond the sound of the pebbles
and the Murphys' dog.

Crump would fix that guy's ass for him. He grabbed his service
revolver, then threw it onto the bed while he pulled on his uniform

trousers. He left the belt and holster there, carrying only the .38, and headed for the front door. He was no fool. He didn't turn his room or porch lights on. His eyes were adjusted to the darkness just like theirs, and he was a cop and had a licensed weapon, and he would be out the dark door and on them like stink on shit.

But his dark-oriented eyes did not catch the length of wire fishing leader stretched across his front steps from one porch column to the other, and he sailed out over his own concrete sidewalk, pistol flying from his grip, and landed on his stomach and chin, unconscious.

When he woke it was daybreak and he was chained to a lamppost in front of the Red Star market, naked, the chains padlocked. He hurt everywhere. He didn't know it then, but the emergency room doctors would find both clavicles broken, plus his nose, his cheek-bones, his jaw. Several of his front teeth had been knocked out. His right arm was broken in two places, his left only once. Both hands were broken, and one of his feet had several broken toes. His knees had been left alone. Doctors guessed the weapon used was a leather-covered blackjack of the type sometimes used to kill large fish.

His head was shaved. His body was tarred with creosote but not feathered. Chained also to the lamppost was a Doberman pinscher that snarled and bared its teeth at him every time he moved or even groaned. Above him on the post was a hand-painted sign: I'M GOING TO STAY RIGHT HERE CHAINED TO THIS POST UNTIL I GET ME SOME BROWN SUGAR.

The police were called, but it was another hour before they could sedate the dog with doped Red Star hamburger and get a bolt cut-ter there to set Crump free, and by then several photographs, both amateur and professional, had been taken. He was hospitalized for a week, and when he was released, the papers were still running the story.

Nobody ever claimed the Doberman. Oddly enough, Crump asked to keep him when he got out of the hospital, and the two formed a strange bond that lasted until the dog's death years later, though he never could be trained. Crump, however, did seem to get the message, and to everyone's surprise he stayed right there on the force, served out his twenty and then ten more—though in a much more modest style than before—and was twice decorated. He was involved in no further racial incidents.

Vic's dad, Uncle Homer, and the Riggins brothers caught no bass that day on Lake Panasofkee, where they'd been fishing for several days and could prove it, but they did bring in several big mudfish—eaters of baby bass—and performed the service of clubbing them with the blackjack to protect the lake's future. Now, it could be argued that bass are themselves dangerous predators, but what the hell, you have to draw the line somewhere.

An envelope arrived for Vic from Mad Moped Max. It contained a check for two thousand dollars. "This should get you started. More if you succeed. Go wherever you want—Juilliard, Berklee, wherever—but the condition is you can't drink for a year." Vic gave it to his mother for safekeeping. In that same day's paper was an article about Max. "MAXWELL GILLETTE, MANHATTAN PROJECT WUNDERKIND, DRIVING FORCE OF JET PROPULSION LAB AND NASA DROPOUT, FOUND LIVING ON BEACH. 'I haven't been lost,' said the man known both for his genius and his eccentricity, 'they have.' Gillette would not comment on the possibility of his rejoining the NASA effort in the new administration. 'I'm working on some things that interest me more. For instance, why don't we use dirigibles? Why do we fear Communists more than pissant dictators like Batista, Trujillo, Somoza, Duvalier? How did Nixon ever learn to play the piano, have children? Why aren't young people listening to jazz?'" Good old Mad Moped Max.

Mr. Branthooven called, a day of surprises. He told Vic with no prologue that he'd been in touch with FSU and they still had a scholarship for him in the Marching Chiefs and concert band. They knew he wouldn't be able to play for a while. He thanked Mr. Branthooven. There was a long pause, then Branthooven said, "Yes, well, good luck."

Vic called him back and said, "I was a jerk. I was lucky to have a teacher like you. You didn't deserve what I did." There was no reply, and he realized eventually that Branthooven couldn't talk. He said good-bye and hung up.

There was a postcard from Baz, more specifically Lance Corporal Basil Belheumer, postmarked Washington, D.C. "USMC, man!" it read. "You were right. Hang on and think of something weird. This was it. No boot camp for musicians, groovy threads, good bread, three squares, hip cats. Come join, man. Like semper fi! Baz."

There was a letter from Kentucky, postmarked before Boop died. "Dear Victor, I want to tell you a few things I've been thinking for your own good. You are not that good. I am not that good. Music, I mean. We are lucky to be like that because it would hurt so much more if we were too good. Because we have been good a few times it could hurt us if we think we can be good enough. Maybe we can be regular people. Don't make such a big thing out of music. Don't make such a big thing out of life. What you snorted was aspirin with a little Miltown. You are all right. Your friend, Elizabeth Burden 'Boop' (Told to Nurse Fontanesi)."

Down Beat

Kenton Blasts Stereo. . . . Kenton labeled the twin-channeled recording and reproductive device "only a gimmick, with no sound musical validity, which will ultimately wind up a fiasco."

Requiescat in Pace, by Leonard Feather. . . . It was probably too much to expect that Billie would survive the self-inflicted beatings beyond the age of 44. Whether the final abandonment of the will to live came with her estrangement from Louis McKay, or with Lester's death, or with the arrest at the hospital, nobody will ever really know. All I know is that to the end Billie for me was the incarnation of soul, of living intensity. She was everything that has ever been connoted by the word *glamour*. She was sweet, sour, kind, mean, generous, blasphemous, loving, and lovable, and nobody who ever knew her expects ever again to know anyone quite like her. For most of us it will be impossible for many months to listen to one of her records without tears. God bless you, Billie.

But Not for Me /

Under the Double Eagle

That next autumn on a football field in Tallahassee, Vic marched with the Chiefs. To be sure, he had no mouthpiece, needed none, was a long way from being able to play, but he was there.

As were his parents and his sister, in the stands, trying to spot him in those crisp ranks of garnet and gold. In the parking lot, his father's Fiesta spinner hubcaps were being stolen. Vic had been humming "But Not for Me" while waiting to come out with the band, and when it began to play "Under the Double Eagle," he reflected that the chords were the same for the first eight bars or so. So the latter martial tune overlapped and then drowned out the earlier Gershwin song as they marched.

But nothing seemed able to make that boy march in step. With the best intentions, he turned right while the band turned left and was, for a while, all alone on the field. He did a to the rear as if it had been planned all along and then, in due measure, rejoined his band.

And on a field far away in the nation's capital, Lance Corporal Basil Belheumer, as if by some telepathic signal, also stepped smartly away from his fellow gyrenes and made the same correction. "From the Halls of Montezuma" follows a similar chord progression.

Back in St. Petersburg, Jimmy Johanssen finally cracked, stole his father's Studebaker Golden Hawk, took it to the new landfill on which his father would develop homesites, and floored it. This once, at least this once, he would find out what it could do. He would have a real V-8 engine roaring ahead of him, pulling him across the sand and shell and sandspurs—a quarter mile in sixteen seconds—and past where he meant to brake, over the seawall, into shallow water at low tide, and to his death.

Far, far away, in Russia, Boris Pasternak dreamed of a giant samovar, lit in neon. Jack Kerouac, napping on Long Island, dreamed of the True Cross floating over the surf at Big Sur. Later—in fact, the next summer—soaked in wine but awake, he would see it again. In New York, Gene Quill felt good for no reason. His horn felt like pure voice, like focused light, like a fountain. He had an invitation from the Hot Club of Japan to play a concert and thought, Man, is this the strangest? In New Hampshire, J. D. Salinger thought he heard someone in his driveway.

"From the Halls of Montezuma" to "Under the Double Eagle" to "But Not for Me"—blended one last time before taking their stories in separate directions.

And far to the north, east, and west, the greasy little horsemen of the Horde let their shaggy ponies graze the steppes and watched the smoke rise from their yurts. Most of their gods were evil forces in their lives, yet they had once conquered nearly all the known world. They trusted only the blue heaven, the spirit of the Great Khan in their yak-tail banner, their horses, and their bows. Now, they were patient in the steppes, deserts, forests, and tundra—waiting for the next coming that the shamans had foretold.

Afterword

When he was eleven, Gene Quill's mother took him to the Steel Pier to meet Jimmy Dorsey, who invited him to sit in on a number and was so impressed that he let him finish the set. Afterward, Dorsey bought Quill and his little girlfriend hamburgers. Gene joined the union at age thirteen. His career peaked in the late 1950s in the several recordings of the Johnny Richards Big Band, and he continued to play through the early 1960s.

He was legendary for his playing, his humor, his temper, and his often self-destructive behavior. There are many Gene Quill stories, but the closest the general public came to knowing his reputation was probably during a "Tonight Show" interview Johnny Carson did with drummer-turned-comic Charlie Callas. When Carson asked Callas what the toughest thing was about being a musician on the road, Callas said, "Rooming with Gene Quill"—breaking up Carson and the band but leaving most of late-night America puzzled. Jim Amaresco told me of Gene sitting on Maury Stein's office couch, in

L.A., heavily self-sedated. He apparently knocked the purse of the woman beside him onto the floor. Gene offered the following punnish apology and explanation: "Pardon me, but it seems I've exceeded my purse-capacity."

In 1967 Gene married Peggy Zangulo, a boardwalk artist in his hometown of Atlantic City, and moved there from New York City. Friends say he had some difficulty adjusting to success and was sometimes hard to motivate. At that remove, his career lost momentum from the earlier time when he was, as his friend Phil Woods put it, "number one call in New York, without flute." He played for a time in Las Vegas and sat in with visiting bands and combos in Atlantic City. He did play with Billie Holiday, Lena Horne, Gene Krupa, Artie Shaw, Claude Thornhill, Quincy Jones, Gerry Mulligan, Michel Legrand, Buddy Rich, and others. There is a legend that he jammed with Charlie Parker at the Welcome Bar in Atlantic City. One of his last regular gigs was there at the Jockey Club, which featured strippers. Like Parker, Quill used heroin or substituted heavy drinking. And, like Parker, he suffered lasting effects (in his case, episodes of epilepsy) from the wreck of a band bus early in his career.

In the late 1970s, while separated from his wife, he was found unconscious in his room. Police said he'd been struck in the head, mugged. Gene remembered nothing. He had brain surgery and lay ten days in a coma. He sustained permanent brain damage and partial paralysis and blindness on his right side, and though he tried to play, he never recovered fully. He spent much of his time in nursing homes. He no longer used drugs or drank. In December of 1988, he had a heart attack. Surgeons installed a temporary pacemaker. He died on December 8, 1988, seven days before his sixty-first birthday.

Billie Holiday died on July 17, 1959.

Charlie Parker died on March 12, 1955.